# Upriver
### PETER MATTHEW BENNETT'S HISTORY

A COMPANION VOLUME TO THE NOVEL
## THE GENTLE RIVER
PROVIDING AN IN-DEPTH BACKGROUND
TO THE HISTORICAL CHARACTERS AND
EVENTS OF THE NOVEL

: : :

## GORDON WILLIAMS

*Upriver*
*Peter Matthew Bennett's History*
Published 2024 by Gordon Williams
Copyright © Gordon Williams 2024
*All rights reserved*

Print ISBN 978-1-8383039-2-1
eBook ISBN 978-1-8383039-3-8



: : :

*Set in 10pt Source Serif Pro*
*Titles set in Cinzel*

*Also by Gordon Williams*


# THE GENTLE RIVER
# SEVEN SHORT STORIES


: : :


www.gordonwilliams.uk

ROSSETTI / BENNETT

PIETRO FILIPPO ROSSETTI (1750-1815) *married, in 1780,*
ANNA ELENA CORELLI (1755-1828) *Genoa, Italy.*
*Their children*
GUIDO (1782-1783)
SANTINO (1785-1787)
PHILLIP (1788-1839, *Captain Phillip Rossetti*)

PHILLIP ROSSETTI *married* JANET WATKINS (1807-1827) *in 1825.*
PHILLIP ROSSETTI *married* CATHERINE PRICE (1802-1863) *in 1837.*
*Phillip and Catherine's daughter*
PHILLIPA (1838-1914) *married, in 1860,*
RICHARD SPARKS (1831-1860);
*their daughter*
GEORGINA (1860-1934) *married, in 1883,*
ARTHUR BENNETT (1859-1942); *their children*
SARAH (1883-1893); RICHARD (1884-1916) *and*
PETER (1885-1942) *Captain Peter Bennett, the Narrator's father*

CAPTAIN PETER BENNETT *married, in 1906,*
ALICIA FRANCOME (1885-1955); *their sons*
PETER PHILLIP BENNETT (1909-1914) *and*
PETER MATTHEW BENNETT (born 1914, *the Narrator*);
*he married, in 1941,* CLARA PORTER (1914-1988); *their children*
PATRICK ARTHUR BENNETT (born 1946)
ELENA ROSSETTI BENNETT (born 1949)

ELENA *married* DAVID LINDBERG (born 1944) *in 1969;*
*their daughter*
ALICE ROSSETTI LINDBERG (born 1972) *married, in 1992,*
JONATHAN ALAN GREERSON (born 1972)

*Also...*
RHIANNON PRICE (1812-1897) *Catherine Rossetti's cousin*
JOHN PARRISH (1788-1858) *Phillip Rossetti's Company Manager*

# CONTENTS

CELYN

BELOW WHITEBROOK, MONMOUTHSHIRE

OCTOBER 13TH 1996

Yesterday I went with my granddaughter Alice to Sea Mills, just downstream from Bristol, and we stood together on the bank of the Avon. The river stretched both ways from us, filled with mist above the muddy low-tide –  grey, desolate, and silent. This was where the ships would pass on their way into the City harbour, and out again to the world –  but now it was back as it was, before eight hundred and more years of commerce and the Romans long before that, before Bristol began. John Cabot sailed past here to the *new founde land* five hundred years ago, and my father's ships a hundred times to and from a much wider world. Our ancestor Phillip Rossetti's affinities with the ways of this river, and the expertise of so many others... his knowledge, and theirs, is lost now and it's all but empty, the big ships gone for ever, the industriousness over with. Alice and I were quite alone on the muddy grass of the bank, and I stared upstream and down, filled again with the emptiness – the lack of everything that used to be. Yet I was also content with its return to its ancient self, and the beautiful calm greyness of the day comforted any regrets I had over the past. Alice said nothing, maybe surprised into silence by the emptiness, and after a while we turned back to the car and left for home.

That was yesterday, a physical step back to the river, and to nostalgia. My real story begins a few miles upstream from here, on a quite different day, long ago, and one perfect to begin with – true, the day at that real beginning was perfect. It had the best sky for me – vast, pale blue and with a few high clouds –  and gentle early-May gusts blew through the streets and shivered the leaves on the trees. It was a day for venturing forth somewhere, for seeing new things, and it began well and happily enough –  a school-free Saturday, and all the daylight hours to look forward to: I would maybe choose to wander down the hill, or maybe not. The world was always fresh for a ten-year-old with much of the close-to-home town and harbour still to explore, and in my black and white memories of 1920s Bristol the streets were different every time I travelled them –  each time something new; small calm shocks to move me, to form memories, to contribute to what we call *life experience.*

Even in those young days everything was colour and light, and shape. My early recollections are of the harbour, of the water rising and falling in the last lock before the river, taking the huge ships with it; of the water lapping at their cold, hard sides and changing with the light, the wind and the seasons. Or the river, dirty brown, connecting the port to the faraway sea, and of the smells and sounds and feelings around me... and the best memory, of Brunel's soaring bridge beyond the lock gates, solid on the clifftops above the river. I would lie far below it, feeling hidden in the tall gorse on the bank and gazing straight up at the high roadway with its invisible traffic and circling gulls, the detail almost lost against the bright sky. I was sheltered and safe, with the bushes around me and the solid roof, albeit spaced far above; it was easy there, no matter what –  my best place on earth in those good, bad, and brief times, before all changed and my hiding-place was lost forever.

I had few friends then, by choice. I was mostly alone, yet truthfully never lonely, and under that bridge was my place of daydreams, but it became the opposite when I would walk out and watch for my father from there on the days of his homecoming, fearing this dream-captain returning and becoming real again. I would watch the ship move quietly by, bringing him home again to Bristol, without him ever knowing I was there. But on that particular late-spring Saturday I was to lose him – not to illness or accident, or carelessness, nothing like that: we would leave each other, we would lose each other. And as this played out, I would feel the distant bridge, but be unable to answer its call.

I am Peter Matthew Bennett, now eighty-two years old, but then a soft boy of ten, a slight gentle boy with the wrong father and too much like my mother, and destined for the old struggle between the disappointed and the bewildered – which is exactly what happened. Most of the ten years before this event, and all the eighteen after to my father's death, were lived in separation from him. *Do we miss, ever or always, those we disliked during their lives?* Some do. Can we become closer to them? Likewise, some do... but most of us end up sometimes thinking well of them, while sadly knowing we don't mean it.

He's before me now, smart in his brass buttons, looking earnestly at the camera. What a nice chap, you might say... such a friendly, self-assured look about him. And faint in the distance, far behind him, is my bridge.

On the perfect morning of that day of our loss I was offered a treat, a gentle treat; a small safe adventure before my seafaring father returned to his seafaring, but sadly I didn't jump at it. But I didn't refuse either so agreed to it by default, which was all I could do, and on that bright and blustery Bristol morning in 1924 my father was to take me down over Brandon Hill to the waterside, to be rowed out in the small boat, out over the deep water of the harbour and under the eyes of the town. I remember waiting by the door, with the sun coming through the glass, and my poor overwhelmed mother pleading quietly with her husband – *Please be careful with him,* she'd said. Missing her meaning in my wish to be elsewhere, what I'd heard was *Take care of my darling boy,* but it wasn't that. It was *Please bring him back alive,* and I know now if I put her husband's thoughts into words I'd have something like, *You stupid woman, what do you know?*

That little boat wasn't new to me – I'd crossed the harbour many times for some reason or other, but that day it was different, it felt open-ended, and there was a strange threat in the air – *you're too sensitive,* my mother would say – *he doesn't mean you any harm. He loves you, never forget that.*

We were drifting under that almost clear sky, and the sun was warm on my hands as we sat facing each other. My father rested on the oars, round face calm and untroubled. The harbour was busy around us but we were ignored, not a part of it, oddly unconnected.

"Stand up, Peter," he said.

His voice was mild, close to gentle, so the impossible words almost went over my head. I watched for him to laugh, to make a joke of it, but as the seconds went by my heart began to quicken. So this was it. No small talk, straight to the point. Surely (so my reasoning went) my antics getting into the boat would have warned him? Had I at last found my sea-legs? Or lost my fear of the water? No, and no: *This little wobbly boat? You know well enough I can't do this.* We floated serenely, an equal distance from anywhere safe.

Again, "Stand up, Peter."

Now he sounded bored; too quiet. And he was looking

out over the water, so said it to nobody until he turned his head back to me.

"*I can't.*"

"Yes you can."

Ten seconds, probably, from security to panic. My fears of the breathless water had gathered, multiplied, and now ranged far beyond simply wobbling over the side – my focus was shifting, and panic made me irrational: there was now the bottom of the boat to think of. Half-an-inch of wood, the thickness of my thumb, and he wanted me to stand on it. My feet would go through the slimy old clinkered boards, followed by the rest of me into the depths of that black lapping lagoon... and what horrors would be waiting, as I shot screaming down before the shocked eyes of my father, leaving a pathetic mound of froth and bubbles? I saw his dim face peering through the hole as I was sucked down away from the sunlight, and wanted to warn him – *Don't do this to me... please. You'll be sorry, sorry you even thought of it.* Such are the wonders of the brain, from maybe to probably to definitely, all fear-driven in a speck of time.

"Come on," he said, "it's not difficult, nothing to be afraid of. Just stand up."

He was wrong there, it *was* difficult. Impossible, even. And by the way, through all the years since, I remember his voice, that day. Through seventy-two years and hundreds of other voices, I remember that one. It was the intolerant, coaxing voice he normally kept for his wife (did this mean I was growing up?) – loveless, persuasive, threatening: *Do this or you'll be sorry,* or, to show his magnanimity, *You would rather do it this way, wouldn't you?* Never shy of admitting to brutality – or *strength* as he would call it – my namesake father, Captain Peter Bennett, was waiting. Let him wait a while.

So: Bristol, 1924. The setting for this little drama was the Floating Harbour – *the Float,* as we knew it – really a piece of the old Avon which the city snipped off for itself in the early eighteen-hundreds, to get rid of the nuisance of tides coming and going. They sealed it up, and connected the loose ends of the dismayed river with a ditch they called the New Cut, a surgical bypass which nowadays ambles through the city traffic and looks as if it had always been there. The Float was less a place of masts and sails then, but rather funnels, smoke and steam, vast concrete box warehouses and bristling crane jibs along the quays. It was my playground and my life. I spent half of all my early days there, in the endless detachments of my imagination.

I lived with my parents, in a grand house on the hill above the harbour. It wasn't big, but one would be cursed for calling it small, so let's say it was a smallish big house on the lower side of the street, and owned by a big man with big money. Captain Bennett was also the owner of two ships, big enough for oceans but small enough to escape through the winding river that fed the landlocked port. He was Master of the *North Star,* and went to the ends of the world with her. I adored that ship, grew up with it, dreamed about it, fell in love with it the way boys sometimes do, without realising. Mysterious, complicated, romantic, black red white with a great yellow funnel (the badge of The Bennett Line – my name – proud in blue, as big as a barn door). And above all, when I was old enough to grasp it, the name: *North Star.* Everything was in that name. The heavens, the earth and all its corners; warmth, and sultry nights; cold, sharp-frosted clear days and heavy, restless oceans: everything, in fact, that I imagined the real North Star to look down on.

As a baby, I watched her from my mother's arms, going soundlessly through the lock, close enough to touch, close enough to silence me with her size. The huge slab side, bigger than anything I'd seen, black-painted, catching the slanting sun as she passed slowly out into the Avon. My mother held me weightless in her arms, waving my arm and hers until they ached, and the faraway figure leaning from the wheelhouse waved back. Ahead of the ship, under the sky-blue arch of that lovely bridge, was the unforgiving river which twisted its way to the Bristol Channel and the endless grey of the North Atlantic. *North Star* was on her way again, and we would have peace for a while, steady peace and communion – the best of times.

*But my father is waiting.*

Firstly – how do I remember him? A big man – as tall as a captain should be and broad-shouldered, his heavy face sun-weathered and beardless, with usually an intense expression, as if trying to be handsome (my mother thought him good-looking, which is only right, but I'm sure it was his blue eyes that dazzled her). I can see him now in his uniform, the navy and the gold, the heavy cloth adding to his bulk somehow, certainly to his importance. It would be difficult to match us – I never grew to be like him in any way, and definitely not in looks; in some perverse swindle of fate my mother gave me her face, and her lightness, and his disappointment never left him. And while it's true he was called handsome by others, from now on I'll describe him as I saw him, and not be moved by loyalties or invented affection: *handsome is as handsome does.*

Seated under the rolling sky in that Captain's outfit (to show he meant business), peaked cap stuck on his melon head, he was a ridiculous Pugwash (I warned you about this – I must tell the truth). When I refused to get to my feet in that little rocking boat – out of fear, not defiance – I began taking apart a dream he'd fashioned for himself – how was I to know? After several childless months at sea, thinking, working it out, he came up with this: he would at last make a man of me, train me in the necessary arts of father and son. It was long overdue, and I would not fail him – he would make me do this. My poor Captain father, adrift with such thoughts. (He once had the son he wanted and needed – only to lose him after five years, the blame for which wrongly fell onto his wife and his mother, that poor dispirited pair, but that story comes later).

I was a sad disappointment – a repeat of dainty Sarah, his poor sickly sister already in her grave at ten years old: *He'll come to nothing, this mockery of a son, this weakling, this queer.* Thus would he rant over and around me in the years ahead, when a full head of steam steered him on his raging course. Through my growing-up years, when I needed a father, what did I get? *Oh, for a strong hard red-blood of a boy* (so his yearnings would run), *a hearty no-nonsense fighter! A swaggering unseasick hero, pirate, taker of women, plunderer of men!* But... *no.* In the early days I ran to my frighted mother, who ping-ponged me back to stand and take it – like a man should, perhaps. He never forgave her for me, for giving him a son of no use to him.

He asked me again to stand up in that little boat, and very soon lost altogether his fragile patience; through my starting tears, he began the familiar transformation. He stood up (an expert) and lifted me with his rough hands. I sat down again. He sat down again.

He leaned forward.

*"Stand up!"* His face close to mine, shouting, deafening me. Lifted up, sitting down, falling down, gripping the timbers of the boat – it must have been an almost silent comedy for those who chanced to look, from the safety of the quays.

I remember going beyond tears, ready for death as I

thought it might be, and when as a final and true gesture he drew back his open hand to hit me but instead held it trembling in the air, his exasperation was complete. I would defy him, become unafraid of him – we both knew it, and the shock of the thought killed us both stone dead.

He rowed back in thunderous silence across the Float, all energy and fury while I sat with clenched fists, staring over the black water, wanting him gone; I think the last warmth for him left me then, never to return, and in that little span of time the ogre's fate was sealed. *(This begins to feel better, in the telling – almost done).*

Captain Bennett left for his ship and his men the next day, all dressed-up, all arrogance, but unable to make something, anything, of this *boy*. So I reinvented him, as a child would, to make him easier to bear. There were periods of two, sometimes three months of living without him while he wandered the oceans in his bread-and-butter trade. He wrote kind letters to my mother, distance softening him into a loving husband, even a loving father; he spoke well of me when he wrote and this was the father I carried around in my heart, an absent wandering hero. Even now in my old age I sometimes feel a sad distress for the man, but it was never enough to let him off, to forgive him.

He died somewhere in the darkness of the Atlantic Ocean – went down with the ship (my beloved *North Star*) in the wartime spring of 1942, caught with a hold full of corned beef while racing for the Western Approaches and the hungry bellies of England. I was twenty-eight years old, and tearful for that proud wasted ship. I wept for her who once filled my baby eyes, for the loss of my dream-father, the blameless crew, and the corned beef.

Now we can move on.

My ancestors were a strange lot, but mostly bearable it seems. Apart from my dire father and his mentor the crazed grandmother Phillipa, who smoked cheroots and breathed fire when nobody was looking, they appear to have been... yes, bearable. Before I leave centre-stage – occupied only on these pages, I modestly add – I will go back to the beginning, and from the small clamouring crowd I choose one who doesn't wave urgently to be noticed. His name is Phillip Rossetti. This man is worthy of some reverence because he built the business that gave the wealth to our family, but I like him for different reasons (not that I am ungrateful, you understand – my retirement has been comfortable). My daughter is Elena *Rossetti* because of him, and he would, I believe, forgive me for what I did in 1955, one hundred and fourteen years after he died in that sunlit room some five miles from where I sit. Oh Phillip, I hope you would forgive me, I hope you're not turning in your grave like the rest of them. But no confessions yet.

He was the third son of Pietro and Anna Rossetti, who grew up five years and five kilometres apart in the wooded Polzevera valley behind the city of Genoa, in the north of Italy. Phillip's father Pietro had moved with his parents to the City harbour to be with his uncle's family, who were shipping merchants. This would be around 1757, a few years after their Austrian invaders left.

It seems that Pietro took over after the death of both his uncle and his cousin – how they died, and how he gained their wealth, is unknown to me, but the outcome impressed my father: *See that, boy – that's business!* (Should I be suspicious of this? Should I jump at anything that impressed him?).

Pietro then sold two ships and kept the newest one, thereby streamlining his business, boosting his capital and focusing his mind. He'd found and married Anna, and everything points to them being happy together as they planned a future of prosperity, without knowing the sadness to come... this is all vague history, coming before the journal Pietro later kept, but it's close enough to how it all began some two hundred and forty years ago, in an Italy ravaged by strife and invasion, a country on the ropes.

So with his father's backing, Pietro built the business in Genoa, Italy that he was to add greatly to in Bristol, England. The sorry tale of the Rossetti's first two sons and the couple's resulting wish to make a new start was told often by my father, who arrogantly thought himself to be the family historian. I should say here that his *True Account of Our Family,* as he called it in his absurd mock-Victorian way of writing, was and is a little spare of the truth. He and his smoke-mouthed grandmother come out of it rather better than anyone else would have allowed (I missed sharing the world with that awful woman by five months, but my mother said I was the better for it).

The *True Account* does however have some value, some truth if you look for it, but you must go beyond the hype and dismiss most of the praise. It's useful for dates and big moments and it's mostly my source for this narrative, but I'm weaving through it like a bloodhound on the scent and taking the opportunity to nudge some of the best china as I go *(out with you, rogue!)* – but being a little more selective than any proverbial bull. And in case you wonder about my selection process: yes, it's biased against my long-dead father's list of heroes, most of whom were of his own ilk. (But do I hear dissent? Do you wonder how I can condemn the makers of my fortune while enjoying same? All I can say to those who wonder is this: I am disappointingly human, and have no answer to that.)

There is also the single patchy journal kept by Pietro from the year of his son Phillip's birth, almost up to his own death in 1815; begun in Italian, and skipping several years altogether, in later times it slides easily in then out of English whenever a word or phrase requires it, so it's a colourful if sparse reference to work with. There are other things – letters, documents, ledgers – all from a treasure trove in the loft of Phillip's future home across the Severn in the Wye Valley, and even a short diary of Phillip's from that time.

Then there were the stories from outside the *True Account:* Chinese Whispers across the years, told and retold, buffed-up in the re-tellings – and I don't know, maybe some were invented. My mother Alicia told me many tales of the Rossettis, some sad, some joyful, but mostly ordinary happenings, and these little things I've used to put some human padding over the already plush, puffed-up bones of my father's *True Account.* So what follows is a ragbag, the stories and memories I have and an elaboration of the specifics as I sniffed them out, but they all lead to the same place – they all lead here, and now – to where I'm sitting. I look south from my window and into the sun, down the river-valley towards Bigsweir Bridge, beyond to the old Inn at Brockweir, and many miles beyond that to our home in Bristol. Our crowded history comes from all those places.

## 2

## OUR CROWDED HISTORY

The first two Rossetti children, Guido and Santino – almost the sum of our knowledge of them –  died in babyhood amid the dark dwellings behind the Genoa quays. They probably died from something squalid, Santino reaching the promising age of one year and eight months. But these particular parents failed to give in to the laid-back expectations of the time: *children die, children are replaced by more children equally likely to die.*

Anna was pregnant again – *please, a boy, a new Captain for Pietro!* – and in anxiety they lifted their eyes beyond their homeland, and were swayed by the promise of England and their child being born there (not at all the perfect option – children died there too, but surely their third son would be blessed!). Mediterranean trade was again in decline, so it sounded safer in an unsafe time, and after all Pietro had a small grasp of the language learned over a few years of muddled gossiping with a colourful English sailor, a frequent visitor. In 1788, in the high summer following Santino's death, Pietro weighed it up. This richly-dressed Englishman – in his journal Pietro calls him his *Ammiraglio*, his Admiral – had wooed him with promises of Bristol, of England: *Excellent prospects for business, a big economy with the world to choose from. A mad King – so what? – at least we're talking about it. You've had the Austrians here, had to sell Corsica, trouble in France again which probably means more trouble for you, and Europe again full of rumours of war.* It sounded better the more he thought about it: England owned a fifth of the world, they talked rather than shouted (or so he was told), and of course the new alliance with Prussia and Holland... we'll go to England. A decent Navy, and thirty-odd precious kilometres of water from France and everywhere else. *Yes, we'll go to England.*

But leaving Genoa, their beloved Genova, *La Superba*, was not easy – the proud, splendid city, the watery-blue skies, the history, their friends, their home for so long – and the warmth! There were so many fears, so many anxieties, so many what-ifs... and *what-ifs* led on to *should-we*. So August became September, and September threatened them with October and the North Atlantic winter; on the brink of turning back Pietro went one last time to his confidant, for some reassurance, a little push maybe... some help. *Tell me again.*

So the Admiral went over it all once more.

Even in their hybrid language the message got through, as it had the first time. He talked again of great wealth from the West Indies just waiting, *waiting*, for anyone who cared to make the long journey across. He knew that Pietro would not carry slaves, so spoke instead of the shorter trip, across to Jamaica or Barbados and back again. The wealth he spoke of was sugar, or it could be rum, or molasses, tobacco or cotton, spices, dyes, even precious timbers – it was all there. Forty days across, he said, and thirty back if you were lucky and the winds were kind, but even if you lost time it was a small problem because of the value of the cargo. So forty there and thirty back, that's about ten weeks at sea plus a couple of months loading and unloading, and you can do that twice a year. And it's a two-way trade – you make money both ways... the colonies were also consumers. His journal is full of questioning at this point, full of uncertainties and doubts, but my father (who also read the journal) had none – Pietro would see the sense of coming to England, and not have doubts.

So after his talk with his Admiral, Pietro was seduced all over again, but stayed a wavering virgin where slave produce was concerned. It was two lifetimes since Genoa had supplied slaves to the Spanish plantations, and they knew that England was in the unhappy throes of stopping it altogether. He and Anna made a faintly earnest promise to each other to avoid the West Indies if they could; but if they were unhappy about where their new trade could come from, they certainly would have seen the possibilities – and as no outright condemnation of slavery came from the Catholic Church, all would depend on conscience. The Admiral was apparently bemused at this: *money is money, and you know, those people are content, they have a better life over there.* Pietro wrote those words down but surely knew better than to believe them, and a compromise was brought about between him and Anna – they would go, and if he could he would find trade other than from the West Indies... the Baltic, or Canada – even the distant east was promising in those days of the overstuffed British Empire. (These early sentiments please me, yet they were naïve. But it's so easy to be critical of another age. When their Admiral returned in early September they were both set on England.)

Pietro's *Ammiraglio* was Captain David Calvet, the grand Englishman who swayed him (who then swayed Anna) into leaving Genoa: his name is there in the *True Account*, with the words, 'A *Gentleman, with a Desirous Fortune, the same Hero who ensured the Safe Arrival of Pietro, Anna & Their Fair Child to our Fair Port'.* That's another way of saying that Captain Calvet convinced the Rossettis that Bristol was the place to be at that time, and the *Desirous Fortune* part was my father being seduced by wealth and anyone who had it... but at least this Captain was the real thing. A lot of digging finds him living in Hotwells, near the entrance to Bristol Harbour, and being very successful. His wealth came from slavery, and built on that of his father (an escaped French Protestant, a Huguenot, from the walled city of Carcassonne, in the South) and most importantly he was a member of The Merchant Venturers, the controllers of the wealth of the port... so a Desirous Fortune he would have had. Genoa was his slowing-down: his money was made, his later years were upon him, and he took pleasure from the leisurely voyages south in those brief warless times, still taking the tainted sugar, and sitting in the taverns and coffee houses, talking with whoever – his Italian must have been better than Pietro's English – and passing the time until his ship was ready to go back home.

: : :

Captain Rossetti readied himself. Before the end of that Golden September all his focus was on departure, and in his mind the far-off land was there, already finding space for him and his growing family, his precious ships, his chosen crews. Those ships, *Firenze* and *Maddalena,* were his life beyond Anna, their lost boys and their promised child. *Firenze* he renamed *Florence* in honour of the English; she was a hard-worked three-masted barque, a big, solid, elegant youngster of eight years, his workhorse that never sailed empty, and the other, *Maddalena,* a much smaller and prettier two-masted schooner. He writes that he bought this pretty one almost on a whim after he fell in love with her as she rode on her leash in the harbour (his wife knew his heart was true, but would have hoped the same for his eyes. Buying a ship for love was the action of a rich enthusiast, not a mature working captain. But I can imagine him saying to her, *she just looks right). Maddalena* was two years old, and fast, ideal for lighter cargoes to be moved quickly up and down the coast. He admits to watching with envy as his friend Luigi Pastore drove her headlong from the harbour out to the Ligurian Sea, sails taut, parting the water like a knife, and I guess he felt like an old man yearning for a sports car. Captain Pastore would take her to England, but would not commit to leaving Genoa for good unless, as he apparently put it, *That place proves to be much better than this place.*

So in that autumn, on the last day of September, *Florence* and *Maddalena* left the old port of Genoa for the last time, flying ensigns of the Genoese Republic (the same as the English Cross of St George – a good omen, surely; they would fly them all the way to Bristol). They carried what they could, and Pietro listed it all on two pages of his journal – chairs plain and ornamental, chests plain and carved, tables round and square, his much-loved Piedmont desk; paintings, gilt mirrors, and their bed; piles of curtains, clothes and bedding, and a thousand other precious things from their lives together in Italy. Their huge walnut armoire was left behind, sold along with the other twenty-five percent they couldn't get on board. All this – and a cargo of silk, velvet and damask.

The schooner was filled to the hatches with perfumes, jewellery, handmade flowers and a large amount of gold lace; *Maddalena* at that point was worth far more than her bigger companion, and a lucky pirate could have retired in happiness if she'd been caught.

The faithful *Tramontana* blew from the hills in the north-east, filled their sails and for the last time went with them westwards towards Gibraltar, where it handed over to the easterly *Levanter* which took them through and into the Atlantic, in fair weather. Anna was far into her pregnancy, and I'm sure more precious to Pietro than the richest cargo he could imagine; they lived in his cabin, and though he would have insisted she rest rather than walk the deck in the wind, a note in his journal tells how she couldn't help herself and had looked back to Italy for many hours, until the hills disappeared in the haze. Two-thousand-odd miles, about eighteen days if all went well. *England in just three weeks.*

But alas the wind turned with the weather, and the ships ran east for cover as they rounded Spain at Cape Finisterre. Maddalena hugged the coast as Florence ran before the wind, further out, thinking to put in at Santander, but the storm eased and they both turned dead north across the Bay of Biscay. The *True Account* says they raced north together, passing Ushant and the Isles of Scilly before entering the Bristol Channel, and it mentions Wolf Rock: *'They heard the howling of the Fearful Wolf Rock, and Their Great Courage did not desert Them.'* In those days this cowering rock had no marker, and when it couldn't be seen the eerie howling from the deep fissures was the only warning – a natural *keep clear.* It's between the Scillies and the furthest west point of England, and they would have gone through, pushed by another storm, forced to run on in heavy seas and maybe in darkness, racing with the current through the gap and hearing but missing Wolf Rock – by how much we'll never know. Pietro's journal only mentions, in Italian, a *'great storm'*, and *'running through the channel too close to England'*, so my father added the genuine drama of Wolf Rock, which they would certainly have passed and most probably heard, and I muse on how that rock could have denied me and all my family – on how close we came, to being snuffed out.

As the storm eased, they followed the North Cornish coast and passed Lundy half a day later; after a few hours they were picked up by a foraging pilot cutter from Crockerne Pill on the Avon, but with the strain of the past days Anna was distressed, and feared for her child. Pietro sent the cutter back to fetch a doctor, with the promise of payment and pilotage into Bristol.

Thus Phillip Peter Rossetti was safely born on a bright October day in 1788, two weeks before his time, in his father's smoky cabin on board *Florence* as she waited with the little schooner at the anchorage at King Road for the tide into the Avon, and Bristol. His father was Pietro *Filippo*, but the child was named, like the ship, to honour the English, and as a splendour of late autumn sunshine came onto them after the days of storms, they adored the special son – am I sounding like my father here? – no matter; they rejoiced, and this was the boy who would survive.

## 3

THE BOY WHO WOULD SURVIVE

Our shaky history records their arrival at Bristol like this: *'And so those ships, the Brave Florence and the Swift Maddalena, came into the Harbour, and the Rich Cargo was seized upon by the many Noble Women of that Area.'* Noble women? I think not father, not at the dockside, but anyway the Ligurian silk, velvet and damask were haggled over and sold, and after a night spent on board they moved into the house they would keep all their lives, sought out and kept for them by their Admiral in the weeks before. It was across the Hotwell Road, on the bank right below Brandon Hill, in Queens Parade; the first in a terrace of tall Georgian houses facing up the hill but overlooking the harbour from the back windows. It soon became *Casa Blanca,* not because it was white outside, but because all the rooms were white – empty walls and ceilings glaring at them, waiting for their touch. It was up-to-date *English,* they were told, so the white stayed. There was a small patch of garden, planted weeks before with sleeping bulbs – crocuses of all colours, found by Captain Calvet in the hills behind Genoa, hoping they would agree to the climate and delight them all in the coming springtime. It seems he was always sure that Pietro and Anna would come to Bristol.

They lived with their new son in the oasis of their house, close to the bustle of the harbour roads and the comings and goings of all manner of humanity; even dead-of-night silence never happened as life and business went on around them, ships coming and going at all hours with the tides. They were used to busy harbour life in Genoa, and would not have liked solitude. But as for healthiness, where they now lived was deceptive: the streets were cleaner, but the drains and culverts that were the reason for this emptied into the Frome and the Avon, the two rivers that were also the harbour. So, much like Genoa, Bristol Harbour was an open sewer – there was always the hope that the tide was taking it all out, but it plainly wasn't. They must have been used to filthy water and the stench from it, and were not much shocked.

Captain Calvet was their friend, adviser and agent all in one. Without their *Ammiraglio* the Rossettis would have stayed in Genoa, and faced the shame of the approaching French empire-building with fortitude, no doubt. But they came, and it was Calvet who prepared the ground for them in every way, and not just finding the house: he set up meetings with merchants, discussed everything with them and talked incessantly, forcing the new language on them both. He was to help them as far as he was able, as far as certain disapproving fellow merchants would have allowed, and the *True Account* inevitably tries to praise both the rich merchants of Bristol and the newly-arrived *Catholic foreigners;* there would have been resistance from high places, but Calvet somehow smoothed the waters for the Rossettis. They would go on to make money, and, of course, to pay their dues. So they settled in, Pietro speaking a sort of English to his hopeful Anna, who tried; he was thirty-eight, she thirty-three years old, and as the days, weeks and months passed they grew into the house, the language and everything else.

: : :

By his early forties, Pietro had taken *Florence* to all the places that would give him the greatest return, including the West Indies. There are hints in his journal that the old pledge to not trade there had become tired by then, and both he and Anna were agreed about bringing the precious cargoes from Barbados and Jamaica. They both knew that slavery would end, but they knew the *fruits* of slavery would always be there.

This was all before the time of the Floating Harbour, and the tides still came and went, leaving ships on the mud twice a day, very unlike Genoa – the Rossettis had come from a city of the sun to a city of the moon. At Genoa they were ruled by the sun, as there was no tide to speak of, and their lives would follow the fixed comings and goings of the light; they could sail in or out any time they chose. Not so with Bristol, which was ruled by the moon; huge tides came and went twice a day, always at differing times, and everything in this port was arranged around them. The rhythm of life and business was very different, and their persuasive Admiral had warned them long before: *It will be strange for you, to be ruled so by the moon.* Pietro thought not much of it. If the Admiral could become wealthy here, he could become more so – moon or no moon.

He must have known the unique problems with Bristol before he arrived: extra to the hassles of the tidal harbour were the perils of getting up or down the river safely. Ships would wait at King Road, outside the Avon estuary, then be off down the river as the tide rose, but without help would soon be in trouble. Left to itself, a sailing ship would run with the current but could not turn easily; the water moving with the rudder rather than over it, making it almost useless as a steering device... the outcome for a large vessel would be to hit the bank at one of the turns, then for the stern to be swept around to the other bank and block the river entirely. The answer for this was to be pulled and guided by rowing boats, keeping the ship to the middle of the river by brute force; these dedicated supermen – *hobblers* – were a vital part of the Bristol scene.

This odd process gave Bristol harbour a poor reputation over the years, and much trade was lost to other ports. The expense, slowness and danger of entering or leaving was the reason for its decline, and only very seasoned mariners would consider a permanent base at the port. Pietro was one of those and quickly learned of the river, the pilots and the hobblers, and through all his time there never suffered the way many did. A few panics certainly, but nothing to really raise the pulse.

My mother told me how the schooner *Maddalena* had been sold soon after they arrived (a sad bow to common sense over the yearnings of the heart), and replaced with *Pensive*, a more sensible and solid ship able to take the bigger, well-heeled cargoes. The journal says that Captain Pastore stayed for half a year with *Pensive*, before he repatriated himself in some disarray – *He misses the sun,* thought Anna... so an English captain was found, and English crews replaced many of the faithful, homesick Italians within two years. Things were moving again for the Rossettis, and young Phillip grew up on the ships and wharves a short distance from his home. He went to sea with his father at five years old, to their delight but to the horror of Anna, who dreamed up endless terrors for her beautiful boy.

And terrors there were, in those days.

The sea itself was hazardous enough when anything much beyond placid, and the workings of those big ships so intense, so hard, so critical, that any carelessness in heavy weather could cost the crew their lives. Pietro knew well enough that a man who has no fear of the sea will soon be drowned, and he treated it with great respect.

There was also the latest war with the French and the constant risk of meeting a skulking privateer even close to home, or a roving press gang coming alongside to take the best of the crew for the King. These things were not new to him, apart from the press gangs, but the lack of those in the Mediterranean had been outbalanced by the risk of attack from the Barbary pirates, looking for cargo and slaves.

These were the closing years of the eighteenth century – the French were having their Revolutionary Wars with all and sundry (but especially the English), and Bristol struggled with change. The trade lost from the Port would not return, but sugar was still the best way to make money there, and everything from tobacco to rum was brought across the Atlantic; by the age of ten Phillip was always with his father aboard *Florence* on the wearisome journeys to the West Indies. During the years of war it was required that ships sail in convoys for safety, but like many others Pietro often chose to pay higher insurance for the freedom to sail alone, to choose his harbours and his routes. A risky business, all in all.

I wonder about Phillip's education, as there's nothing written about it. I had stories from my grandmother Georgina about him and wish I'd written them down (he was her grandfather, but she arrived too late to know him); I was twenty when she died and must have had other things on my mind. One memory though – *the Rossettis, being Catholics, could not find a school for him.*

Those were the tail-end years of real Catholic suppression, but all cities in England still had their share of haters of Popery. So I think of the Rossettis keeping themselves quietly to themselves, and finding (as she thought likely) a private tutor for their son, no doubt with Captain Calvet's help (and we must anyway assume Calvet had no problems with their religion, which is surprising, given his family's history with Catholic Carcassonne). But what of those long voyages? Month after month away from home, away from that plausible tutor, learning of the sea and its ways but not much else? Well, I can also see Pietro taking a tutor with them, someone to distract the lad from the endless round of on-board duties and pleasures and give him an education, which he had for sure because I have a letter, kept in its faded envelope, written in the 1830s to his second love, my great-great-grandmother at Brockweir in the Wye Valley, and that letter shows an educated Phillip. It's a nice thought, to be taught at sea.

The Rossettis would have found the one place in Bristol to worship, which was a mile away at St James's Back, in the upper room of a warehouse. They would have gone there until the first proper Catholic church opened, closer to them, a couple of years later. So, while never losing their wariness, they mixed, they socialised, and they integrated.

: : :

The outbreak of war with France in 1793 was the beginning of the end for Bristol's slave trade, but Phillip's father Pietro still brought home the sugar the slaves produced. During his early years there he'd watched the slaver *Pilgrim* leaving on the tide, described by my father: '*So Pietro watched in Admiration as the Worthy Pilgrim sailed from the Harbour, intent on another Voyage of Excellent Profit.*' He'd seen her being loaded in the days before with glassware, woollen cloth, brandy and allsorts made of iron, brass and tin, all to pay the native slave traders. Unbeknown to him at the time (or to my unbothered father ever, I wonder, in vain) she was to take four hundred and twelve Africans away from the island town of Bonny, and come home five months later packed with sugar and molasses: that's real history, and a fine use of the name *Pilgrim*.

The Trade was further back in Pietro's mind now, but he talked to his young son, trying to explain the inhumanity of man, and kept selling his sugar as the century turned; amid the troubles of war he traded well with both ships, sometimes going north to Canada for timber. The Rossettis were now very settled, the house was as they wanted it and business was good, *Florence* and *Pensive* more than earned their keep, and Pietro's contacts were wide in the cosmopolitan port.

Their friend and saviour Captain Calvet had died in 1802, and he willed them one of his ships, *Wakeful*. *(Apparently this captain of slavery was also a thoughtful gardener; how easy to be won over by this softness, and overlook the other side to the man. No, I'm not forgiving, even knowing how he helped the Rossettis. Those times were different, I know... and he wasn't a novelty – every age has people like him. So I thank their Admiral, and condemn him, in unequal measure).*

*Wakeful* had been a slaver through Bristol's busy years in the Trade, but was converted from a specialised people-carrier by Calvet, and spent her later years bringing timber from Riga and Tallinn. Pietro worked her for a year then sold her, finding three ships vastly more work to manage than two, especially with Bristol's high running costs. The money he had from the sale of *Wakeful* he put aside, *for a rainy day,* he said. I can see Anna reminding him of the rain outside their window, and them both becoming wistful for the sultry blue of Genoa.

: : :

The early eighteen-hundreds were big for Bristol, because during those years the Floating Harbour arrived, after a quarter of a century of dithering. It was a simple idea: seal off the river through the port to keep the water in, so the tide was always high and ships could be loaded or moved any time. Locks were built at each end, and the river diverted to the south, joining its old self again a couple of miles to the east.

Phillip was twenty-one when it opened and the river was let into the New Cut, when the gates of the harbour were closed, and the water was high and stayed there – a novelty for the hundreds who watched the event, not quite believing their new harbour. Bristol would be helped by it, but soon Liverpool and Glasgow would have the edge and the harbour would begin its slow, hundred-and-seventy-year slide towards leisure and the final steps away from a working port. But not yet. Life was changing for Phillip; he was now master of *Pensive*, his father handing her over to him two years before, he continuing with his beloved *Florence*. Pietro was almost fifty-nine, feeling the long years in his bones, and fearing his working life was ending.

So at the age of nineteen, Phillip Rossetti had become Captain of *Pensive* (a pensive Captain indeed) and this began the time of change and development for the family – my family. The change was immediate, and final for him; the headstrong new Captain would have no more to do with the West Indian trade, and would buy nothing produced by slavery. His father was dismayed, but had feared it was coming, and blamed himself both for using the Trade and for convincing his son of its cruelties – a self-tied knot he couldn't undo.

For Phillip, the final truth of the horrors had been at

Kingston, Jamaica, when he was thirteen. He'd left the harbourside to look around that strange place, but returned before long, then stayed on board until they left for home, having seen the worst of humanity along the dirty side roads of the slave port. We don't know what he saw, but it was enough to turn him away for ever.

My father wrote: '*He wandered a short way through the Town, and was stopped short by his Youth; his Character was forming & He would harden as the years went by. So He was kept on board by his Father until their Voyage Home*', then, later: '*Phillip saw Greater Gains away from the Indies, and Won Business taking Goods other than the Sugar that made Their Great Fortune.*' Now my father would not be pleased by him giving up the sugar trade, but he could not be honest and disapprove of what Phillip did. It seems no shadows were ever allowed to fall over the family or its business. Anyway, the boy was turned away from any links to slavery, and I imagine Pietro in his cabin talking to him, trying to justify his business there, and Phillip in some confusion and shock over what he'd seen. My own father would put it down as a good character-building exercise, and he would be right – but the boy's character would build on a different path to his. Captain Bennett simply adjusted to this, and would claim a financial reason for Phillip's change of direction – *More money here than there,* he would say, *simple as that, no mystery.* Captain Rossetti just followed the money. Well, he did, and he made it work without the guilt that his father felt, and which mine would never feel.

But yet again, I find myself trying with my father. Trying to see some good in him after all the years of separation, after his lifetime of being so different from someone I could love, so different from my dream-father. How could this happen? Was he really the brute he seemed to be? I think hard of the years of his wasted life – wasted to me, that is; an intelligent and clever man, yet he chose his path and became mad with those he should have loved, and who were always open to him even after years of abuse. *But no, that's wrong, I'm no long-suffering saint.* True for my mother maybe, but not for me. Would I have taken him back, welcomed him as a changed man, a loving father at last? It would have been hard, so probably not, if I'm honest. But still she'd try: *You're too sensitive, he doesn't mean you any harm. He loves you, never forget that.*

I saw a few brief flickers of something in him, not love for me but something I could warm to, a short-lived one-way rapport, if you like. He always preferred to walk from our house up to Brandon Hill, then down through the trees and across the grass to the Float (as we did on that terrible Saturday) rather than take the shorter route down Park Street, all downhill, but all paved, all unnatural. A small thing maybe, but not when I'm looking for *any* softness in him. And I also saw him several times – hands in pockets, head back – looking up at the stars, as I loved to do; did he see what I saw? Was this a soft side to him perhaps, a dreamy side? I doubt it. On still, bright nights, with the wide heavens above me, or on rough nights, all wild with stars, I would be besotted by nature... but I think my cold father only observed the stillness or the wind and looked at the stars for affirmation, as if checking his compass, as if checking Polaris was where it should be – that's the only side of him I ever felt I knew. But did he really see beauty there, and hide it all his life? If so, he hid it well.

## 4

## SHIPS & CARGOES

Pietro Fillipo Rossetti died on June 17th 1815, the day before Waterloo and four days after falling into the harbour from a little boat – *I would have warned you about this, Pietro* – and coming down with something potent from the filthy water, maybe the same sickness that had taken his boys. Crossing the harbour for him would have been as simple as walking along a road for us, so quite what happened, I don't know. Maybe he stood up too quickly, became dizzy, and lost his balance... whatever, he recovered straight away and pulled himself back onto the boat, but not before swallowing some of that putrid water. I guess then it was dysentery, often fatal in those days. This extraordinary tragedy for Anna, to lose him as they both expected an easier life must have been hard, especially as the French Wars were about to end for good, and the world was calming down and opening up for their son. I can imagine Phillip's distress, and his feelings as he took command of *Florence*, their favourite ship.

We can move on through these years, when Captain Rossetti came into his own and flourished, sailing everywhere profitable. Sugar still made the most, but apparently he never touched it; likewise cotton, rum, molasses or tobacco – all from slavery. He specialised in timber, from Canada and Newfoundland, Sweden, Finland and the Baltic states; from Archangel in Northern Russia, and even the Far East.

Shortly after his father's death he'd found John Parrish, a fellow his own age, and recruited him as manager, accountant, agent and supporter to replace Pietro, who'd been all of those things. They were both fired-up at the prospect of new and easier business as the wars ended, and looked to buy more ships; as the European navies wound down after Napoleon's demise there were many solid and cheap ex-navy transports for sale, and in September 1815 Phillip bought two of them: *Horace* at Portsmouth, and *Montclair* at Morlaix (a river port, like Bristol) in Brittany. *Horace* changed gender and became *Anna Elena* after his mother, but *Montclair* kept her name.

His time at Morlaix, straight after the war, is intriguing: there were several voyages there, and John Parrish suspects an ulterior motive for further visits, but we know no more than that – and I cannot begin to piece things together with such a lack of information. Did he find someone there? A romance perhaps? Later, when writing about Phillip's first love, John Parrish observes *'I have seen Him but once before like this,'* which is a clue which sadly leads nowhere. We shall probably never know, but whatever, he would still have been the enemy to most French. We know he spoke a little of their language, and it appears they were happy to take his money. He sailed off with one of their ships.

Phillip still lived with his mother at *Casa Blanca,* even though in 1814 his father had bought a new property – my growing-up house, a hundred years later – for their son in Charlotte Street, on the hill above the harbour, probably in the hope that he'd marry and settle there. But as there's no hint of female company at that time he was no doubt lonely in that house, and soon moved back to the dockside. After his father's death he rented it out, presumably with his mother's blessing – she would surely be happy to have him back; he would stay with her through his best years, off and on, until her death.

Those years from 1815 were spectacular for Phillip Rossetti. With four ships, he perfected his trade from the corners of the world, from Canada to Finland, from Spain to India and Ceylon, from anywhere that grew the timber he needed: softwoods like spruce, fir and hemlock from the north, and the exotic hardwoods – teak, rosewood, mahogany, ebony and padauk from the tropics.

John Parrish, Phillip's jack-of-all-trades, did everything except sail with the ships. He managed, accounted, helped and encouraged everyone from captains to boys to work well for Phillip. He could be left for months on end in his office on the quay, a safe pair of hands and with a rare talent for working with people. Captains and crews came and went, with a constant whittling down of abilities until the right men were found, and after two years of having four ships the system was working. He shared Phillip's sensibilities (but not his Catholic faith – which seemed not to matter to either) and together they transformed an already good business into an excellent one. They specialised, and simplified: government stores, glassware, wool, even coal, went out from Bristol, but only timber came back, and they had a glorious ten years.

All of this is surmised from the records and accounts of the time, held by my father in his panelled office looking out over the harbour, and only freely seen by me or anyone else after his unexpected death; they would be useful to me fifty-eight years later (his entire lifespan of years later) when I put this story together.

While it's true that Phillip was high on Captain Bennett's list of heroes, it's also true that John Parrish wasn't. He carries the blame for his own and his master's moral stance on slavery, and he's constantly berated for missing the extra profits from the Trade while the Hero is forgiven for having the same *faults*. There's just one memorable point where he's given faint praise – which is then made fainter: *'John Parrish was of some help to Phillip, but with a small Appreciation of the Necessities for Good Business.'* My father's grandmother Phillipa would in time abuse this poor man's expertise and loyalty, and she alone would form her grandson's opinions of him. That the Owner and Manager together raised the business much higher than the Owner could have done alone, is ignored.

From my delvings, John Parrish was a godsend – a very able man, a happy father of two young girls, and clearly having the skills needed to help Phillip. Although Phillipa would condemn him, the facts are that the business doubled its profits during his first ten years (*'...and the Genius of my Grandfather was clear to all who looked Enviously upon Him'*) – and that would not have happened had he been any less than competent. Our *True Account* has been unkind to John Parrish, but when Phillipa took over in 1863 – long after Phillip's death – the ground beneath her was set firm and profitable, mostly by his efforts. She was to reward him according to her character.

: : :

Phillip Rossetti was an unlikely blend of hard businessman and dreamer, an idealist who fought for his beliefs, but not often to the cost of others, it seems. There were many working men in Bristol ripe for exploitation, as times were hazardous to everyone seeking work or help for their families. Men were thrown out for the slightest weakness, and easily replaced from a sea of willing hands. Poverty surrounded the port, and heroism was everywhere – lives were risked and given up for loved ones, but these things were casually ignored by the Owners and Masters, who in their turn had to be successful: the old difficulty of balancing kindness and shrewdness. I'm certain Phillip managed that trick, and became wealthy by it.

My father, while praising everything Phillip did, was often sadly untruthful while doing so. He couldn't bear to have him appear less than ruthless, so he simply lied through most of the *True Account* – '*Captain Rossetti had Great Success with the Shipping of Native Rosewood from South America, though it is true that he failed to capture the Bristol market owing to the Violence of His competition in the Port.*'

That violence is just one example of his perversity – a falsehood to cover the fact that in 1817 Phillip turned away from putting another timber importer, Josiah Ashford, out of business, which he could easily have done. He actually worked with him, rather than take his trade away, and I believe he never had ambitions to *capture* the Bristol market. Those sentiments are in documents and letters my father would have read, but felt needed ignoring, or at least improving. And therein lies the danger of his *Truly-Less-Than-True Account*.

## 5

## BROCKWEIR

This story now looks northward for the first time, for while the world turned in Bristol, something sent Phillip away across the Severn on a journey that would in time change everything for him, and for us – the beginnings of the Brockweir connection.

In 1820, at thirty-two years old, five years after starting with John Parrish and in the middle of their boom years, Phillip Rossetti left Bristol, crossed the Severn, and walked north through the Wye Valley from Chepstow. It was a break, a respite for him, first suggested by John but then grasped in his own mind, an almost unthinkable thing to do: he would trust his ships to his manager, and rest his mind in some solitude. Unthinkable, because a man's place was with his business, not with some dreamy escape to the country. He went, in early June, and kept (to my delight) a slim pocket-diary which he'd begun the year before, and which held his secret wish to do just that – to go away from Bristol and find a place for himself and his dreamt-of family, to give up the sea and run his business from wherever he settled; his friend John had been perceptive, and suggested the beginnings of the very thing he secretly wanted.

The diary included the three weeks he spent walking alone. He was to return refreshed that same month, having discovered and bought a run-down building just over the river from the village of Brockweir, halfway between Chepstow and Monmouth. John Parrish was amused by his Captain moving into property, and Phillip's diary is honest: *'I have done this thing, but only from My*

*Heart, which is now shared between Bristol & Brockweir. I am not able to hold it up as a good Investment of my Money, but I cannot help but take notice of the Happiness it provides Me.'* Don't wonder whether my father disliked this wayward seed planted by John Parrish – even though the ruin would in time become his growing-up home, and profit him greatly in the years ahead.

Just beyond the crossing at Brockweir, the ruined cottage was set back under the wooded hill on the western side of the old coach road from Monmouth.  The outlook was across the Wye to England, the rising ground lifting the eyes to the sky. This was, as Phillip discovered, the remains of *Lower Carreg,* a small house left alone for the past thirty years, and unlived in for at least fifty. It had the English-Welsh pairing in its name, a common enough trait in any border country, and which he found inspiring: *'The Name gives Hope that the 2 intolerant Nations can share & live together, & I am Heartened by it.'*

As soon as he saw it, tucked almost into the hillside, he felt it was there for him to rescue, to replace the tumbledown sadness with a place of refuge for him. He writes of his dismay at its neglect in surroundings of such beauty, and I think the splendid summer of that year helped his decision to buy the ruin and much of the bank behind it, to the top of the hill. The warmth must have played a part, and mellowed him towards what the owner suspected was unsaleable, because Brockweir in those days was a wild place –  a small gathering of cottages and boarding houses, with no church and apparently some sixteen inns, all catering for the rough types who worked at the quayside, loading and unloading the ships and barges. 'Probably the most lawless place in England', I once read somewhere, so even though Phillip's dreams lay a few hundred yards beyond and across the river from the village, it would be tainted by the misrule there, hence the unsaleable tag. He was not put off by it, even after sensing the local feeling of 'one born every minute'.

The village's success was from small-scale boatbuilding and the steady work of transferring goods from ship to barge and vice versa – Brockweir is the highest part of the Wye reachable by ship, so any goods going further north would be transferred to barges, or trows, to be hauled up to Monmouth and beyond. Likewise, most cargo coming south by trow from Monmouth and even Hereford would be put into ships at Brockweir for the onward journey to the Severn, and then – usually via Bristol – to the world.

The village and its quays were cut off from Phillip's cottage by the river, supplies coming in by ship and donkey-cart on the English side. Brockweir was thus largely self-sustaining, but he would still need to be careful to keep an eye on his property during its planned salvation, as sometimes a few of those unsavoury types would cross for the short journey down to Tintern, or up to Llandogo, passing *Lower Carreg*.

He needed another John Parrish to look after things while he was away, which would be most of the time. This man would need to be honest and hopefully tough, to deal with any threats from over the river, and during the bargaining for the cottage with the owner of *Carreg*, the big house on the hill above, he was introduced to George Watkins, their estate manager. George was allowed to split his time between the estate and the cottage – and in a few year's time would offer Phillip the great treasure of his daughter's hand in marriage; she was to be Phillip's first love.

So the builders came, and stayed for nearly three years. I think George would have vetted them well, and mostly left them to get on with it, but we know he also had a watchman on site, presumably armed, such were the times. Three years, during which the ruin was replaced by a house with potential, for the absent dreamer. They cut into the bank, spread the new walls towards the road, and raised it with a first floor until finally the roof made it complete, an empty waiting shell, and in the autumn of 1823 Phillip came with ideas of colours, furnishings and furniture, intent on making some future use of this new home.

Those journeys to Brockweir became routine for him, apart from the Severn crossing, which was fraught with danger. This was the Old Passage from Aust to Beachley, used since Roman times, and the graveyard of many travellers; one long mile of rough water, racing tides and small boats, all together a bad combination, and Phillip refused the crossing whenever things looked wrong. He preferred to wait, being a sailor himself, and trust his own judgement. A few years later a steamboat would start there, and the crossing became safer, but was never *safe*, so he shared the dangers and delays and expected to travel all day from Bristol to Brockweir, and it often turned out that way, but he always made up time in his hired carriage, a fast cabriolet, on the last leg north from Beachley.

From that time on, Brockweir vied with Bristol for the attention of this unlikely businessman – so successful at his work, yet longing for something else. My father knew what it was he wanted, but would not tell it to anyone for fear of admitting to softness in the Hero – put simply: Phillip Rossetti longed for a family. Not damning in itself of course, but laudable, or at least tolerable, to want a family – providing settling down did no harm to *The Business*. My father did just that – producing me as a result – but he would never say he settled down... more true that he simply decided to marry and have, hopefully, a son to follow him, to flatter him as the son grew to be like the father (in our case those hopes went awry, to say the least).

So Phillip would also want a son, to follow him, presumably, and thirty-five was a good age to marry, a good age to turn briefly away from a successful business and look for a suitable *younger* woman. At least that was thought a sensible way of doing things; a son would be of a useful age when his father went past fifty and thought of slowing down. Phillip probably carried these needs around with him for a long time, but I feel safe to say he wouldn't marry just to suit his business. Everything points to a deeper need, and I'm happy to embrace that.

Phillip's mother Anna was to live five years beyond this time, aware that her son's heart was really in two places. He lived mostly at *Casa Blanca,* staying at Brockweir for a week here and there, often taking her with him. We don't know what she thought of country life; I imagine the village across the river horrified her with its beerhouses and cockfighting, its total lack of decency and godliness. But the river was a capable defence from all that, and there's no record of any trouble at *Lower Carreg*.

And then, a couple of years later, when the house was settled and lived-in, the meeting took place that would in time take Phillip away from the sea for ever, the longed-for meeting with his first love. *Lower Carreg* was comfortable and there were always helpers (*servants*, I should say) around, and in the summer of 1825 one of these won the heart of the owner –  with a single glance, my mother always reckoned. She was Janet, that daughter of George Watkins, eighteen, also a little headstrong, unspoken for – and beautiful, of course. Phillip thought her to be his long-sought treasure, the direct result of his dreams, and she went from servant to her Master's Beloved in a joyful and genuine rush, by all accounts. All this we can gather from the historical fact of his happiness at finding her (his diary was conveniently added to over the years ahead, but patchily, like his father's journal had been; without these sources this story would be bereft, and largely imagined). Apart from his own writings I have a letter John Parrish wrote to his mother in Gloucester shortly after their meeting and Phillip's return to Bristol, where he says, *'My Employer is beside himself with the unmistakable joy of one who is in love. It cannot be otherwise. I have seen him but once before like this, but I consider this to be different for him. He is not himself, & any business is not safe in his hands, so I gladly carry the burden for us both. He will recover, & return to us presently.'*

: : :

George Watkins, always alone with his thoughts as he walked the estate above the cottage, was delighted with the news. He invited Phillip to Tintern, where he'd lived with Janet since his wife Emily had left them, 'for a rough forester'. One wonders how regretful Emily would be after hearing her daughter was likely to be betrothed to a wealthy property-owning Merchant Captain from Bristol, and whether the rough forester lasted... I don't think she ever returned, but nothing more is known of her.

Phillip visited Tintern when he could, and took Janet to Bristol, showing her off and ignoring the odd inevitable comments about her lowly upbringing. We know she stayed at *Casa Blanca*, and we know nothing of any improprieties there or anywhere else. He was a lapsed Catholic, and she was a Church of England Protestant;

Phillip writes of 'A Foundation of Faith' between them, and there seems to have been no real barriers to their closeness. A little unusual, I think, for the day.

Phillip's less-than-devout connection to the Catholic Church is interesting, given his devout parents. He seemed to take on a different perspective, an altered view of life and the weight put on it by religion – for better or worse – and came out with an intolerance of all the allowed injustices around him. He would no doubt be hurt by the Pope's lack of condemnation of slavery... a lack also seen in Bristol, where many notable church people were wealthy via the Trade, and where prayers were offered in churches built with money from slavery. He was too tender for his time, perhaps, and held onto a basic faith without the layers of hypocrisy he saw around him.

His mother Anna, now seventy-two years old, while largely pleased with her son's choice, would surely be upset over Janet's religion. But Phillip was thirty-seven, and in her eyes desperately needed to marry before becoming *un vecchio gentiluomo,* an old gentleman, as she'd reputedly often reminded him – in Italian and English – once he'd turned thirty. The religion conflict would slowly resolve in her mind, especially as she could accept that Phillip was not a devout Catholic, but rather just an honest man with Christian virtues. She would cope better with his absence from Mass, and with the wedding, when it came. At least the girl was not ungodly, like the heathens over the river at Brockweir.

During the rest of that year of 1825, through September and October, Phillip took his lady out in his carriage, sometimes driven for him, but sometimes just the two of them. They toured the Wye Valley from Chepstow northwards, climbing the steep road through Whitebrook – along the road that passes my garden – then dropping down to Monmouth, crossing the river there and coming down the English side as far as the coach road would take them. *'Much Delight is had in these Journeys,'* he wrote, *'much Enjoyment, shared and Looked Forward to.'* He mentions many things familiar to me – the views from the Lydart, the extraordinary climb to the Banqueting House on the Kymin Hill above Monmouth, and the many riverside meadows below the glorious autumn colours of the woods. It was after one of those journeys, on the twenty-third of October that year, that Phillip asked George Watkins for the hand of his daughter, and afterwards planned for their marriage at Bristol the following spring.

## 6

## MY RELEASE INTO THE WORLD

To digress: at the age of thirteen I decided to be an artist. Not just an ordinary artist – a portrait painter; forget about arms and legs, or landscapes... *faces* were to be my thing.

My Captain father was less than delighted to hear this, even in jest from my disloyal mother, and laid into me at the dinner table. What was she thinking? Was he going to be happy with that news? I may as well have announced becoming a ballet dancer. So I boldly left the table and risked him following me, went to my room and floated away, away from his fading voice below, to where I could be at peace with my wishful thoughts and plans. I often really thought of running away, but instead imagined it so successfully that I ended up with a parallel life, one where things always went well for me, and my desires were always fulfilled. And anyway an artist, they say, must sometimes have his head in the clouds. He has to be detached, and stand back from the rest of humanity to be able to represent it truthfully. While not being sure of the absolute truth of this, there's no doubt that my head has been detached, in a manner of speaking, for at least half of my life, though not usually when I'm working. And I still have that escape, that daydreamed place, somewhere above and away from reality. This has always been a blessing and a curse, because while it's enabled me to turn away from painful things, it's also stopped me engaging with people and life when I really should have. There was always somewhere for me to run to, somewhere even safer than my den under the bridge, a place where nothing could harm me.

I discovered that place, or rather it discovered me, after the morning with my father in the little boat, when *everything* looked hopeless, even the frail refuge of my mother. Something lifted me away and out of my predicament, out of the presence of these people who couldn't help me, and held me in a cloud of hope. An analyst would probably say I shut down emotionally, as the only way out of an impossible situation, and daydreamed my way to safety. Sounds about right.

Eighteen Charlotte Street was our home, the house Phillip Rossetti's father bought for him in 1814. Part of the late 1700s expansion at Brandon, just off the lower fringes of Clifton, it was a typical square detached Georgian affair without much decoration to its yellow stone walls, and smaller than the row of tall town houses that faced it from across the street. My troubled father always resented this, even trying to buy one of those houses and move across to what he thought was the more fashionable side, but it never happened. So we sat in their shadow as their top floors gazed over us to the harbour beyond.

I was happy there though, with the big rooms and high ceilings; it was almost always warm, and my room at the front looked up at the houses my father couldn't bear to see. His study was at the back, overlooking the Georgian terraces below to the harbour. He liked to keep an eye on things, and would watch the comings and goings through a brass telescope mounted on a stand next to his ornate desk (the more ornate the better, for him).

As a family, we had left the Catholic faith behind with the death of Phillipa, my father's awful grandmother, who herself renounced it (and all religion) from early in her life and was 'entirely free of it' – her own words – in her later years. My father was not religious, except when it suited his purpose, when he could appear to be pious. My mother Alicia was religious, a Baptist from a wealthy family who kept her faith in the face of her husband's railing against religion in general –  a brutal trait from his grandmother. She was always saddened to see him so easily put on his cloak of piety for funerals or weddings or important Christenings, his bowed head fooling no one who really knew him. So I was never pushed into church, but I well remember the pull from my mother and the opposite pull from my father, leaving me on the middle ground where I've settled, unconvinced of either direction, and quite content, so far.

After my schooldays in Bristol, which were uneventful, unmemorable and *long*, I prepared, at eighteen years old, to leave home. This was to be my release into the world, the beginning of my life's journey. I was to study painting – *portrait* painting, at the Slade, in London. To do this I had to go through the normal Fine Arts process, to get a grounding and a feel for things, from charcoal to chalk to watercolour to oils, and everything in between. But I would surely end up as *Peter Matthew Bennett, Portrait Painter.*

My father had long given up on me, but was predictably content to pay my extravagant fees. The Slade was reckoned the best in the country, so he really did indulge me that time. My lodgings also were a cut above – I was given a room in a friend of the family's town house just around the corner from the College, on the top floor of a Georgian terrace, like the houses I looked out at from my window in Bristol, and I was spoiled with all of this.

My mother wept when I left from Temple Meads, standing alone amid the noise and steam as my train chuffed away, waving for ever as she and I did all those years ago when *North Star* left to sail the world. This was 1932, Europe was uneasy, and so many were in hardship and out of work, but my dreamy head was away from all that, and as I was welcomed into my room in Taviton Street, London WC1, I felt on top of the world, free at last from painful parents and tiresome schoolmates.

: : :

The years went by for me in a rush of creativity, a full-on adventure for all the senses I hadn't used in my school years. And of course, there was Clara. I first met her in our second year, in the corridor between *History of Art* and *Figure Drawing,* and the attraction was instant, at least for me; in my usual way I decided to marry her, probably soon after we'd finished at the Slade.

But between that decision and our marriage there were unthought-of trials. It never occurred to me that she may not want me – and this was from naivety, not arrogance – so it was a surprise when I found I had to work towards our certain shared destiny. I had to arrange accidental meetings, and think of impressive things to say; she was bemused, I think, but didn't avoid me. We got together after about two months of this, and after I'd had quite a bashing from the pains of unrequited love.

The years after college were busy for us both, but we shared a lot of time as we followed our ambitions; Clara was into landscapes as fervently as I was into portraits, and as she lived with her parents two streets away from me there were only a few days when we didn't meet, and even fewer after we'd found a studio to share. I took her to Bristol – usually in the spaces between my father's homecomings, just to be safe – and showed her around. My mother was impressed, especially as she was selling her work more often than I was selling mine... she also offered us a room with her (if we married, that is) but that place was beyond the pale for me. We lived with Clara's parents for almost five years, in separate rooms, while everyone wondered were we serious or not. We were, but it took us three years to become engaged; London was an easier place to live together while apart, as it were, and her parents were typical of the arty set whose morals were more allowing towards two people who obviously got on well.

We were married in Bristol in late November of 1941, in St Stephen's Church, somehow missed by the bombs. We looked for happiness while surrounded by the despair of those awful days; the ruins around the city centre, and even up along Park Street towards the house in Charlotte Street, were impossible to ignore. My mother was with us, but my father was not; he was at sea now for most of the time as part of the continuous convoy movements across the Atlantic and back. I think I would have tolerated him on that day in his Sunday Best, but it couldn't be and I never saw him again. He was to die the following spring, an ill-fated component of yet another convoy, the victim of an unknown German U-Boat. I'd seen him twice in the year we were married, but briefly both times, and he was charm itself to my lovely Clara... a man of diverse shades, of course.

We went back to London, and into a different level of destruction. Shortly afterwards I was called up, choosing the Royal Army Medical Corps, not wishing to become a proper soldier; I was to travel Europe for the next three years and see much misery, while Clara moved in with my mother in the summer following my father's death in 1942. I returned – like everyone else, a somewhat changed man – and grateful that she was the same person I'd left behind those three years before.

As peace returned, we settled into Charlotte Street to live with my mother for her remaining years, and by the time our son Phillip arrived in June 1946 we were both selling our work from a shared studio off Park Street. The house itself had no bare walls anywhere (apart from my father's study, which was preserved), as my mother was gracious enough to allow us to cover them with paintings, and not to complain ever about the bad ones.

Clara and I were doing what we enjoyed. I often think of our suiting each other as my greatest blessing, and she still visits me in the only way she can, in my dreams, now and then.

7

## JANET

In the spring of 1826, Phillip Rossetti and Janet Watkins were married. A hired coach took them from Bristol to Gloucester – Phillip refusing to risk his new wife to the ferry and the vagaries of the Severn – a huge but safe detour into Wales where they spent two weeks at *Lower Carreg*. He wrote, *'This place is Best for me, & I hope for Janet, as it improves on any Foreign place I have visited. We are Happy here'.* According to my father (and for once he's telling the truth) he'd had a pendant made for their wedding day – a medieval sailing ship, an imaginative attempt at *Matthew,* the ship John Cabot took from Bristol to North America so long ago, pierced from silver and on a silver chain, delicate, and beautiful. This necklace was placed around his wife's neck as they stood together first as man and wife, and it has been passed down to all but one of the Rossetti brides since that day; my daughter Elena kept it until her own daughter Alice's wedding in 1992, and Alice will hopefully pass it on in time.

They had married in the Captain's Cabin on board Phillip's ship, in the same room where he'd joined the world that bright October day thirty-eight years before. *Florence* sat at her mooring, a step out from the rough bank that was the Mardyke quayside in those days, and the cabin was full, with friends and family squeezed into the space; Phillip's mother was stoical but happy during the ceremony, and Janet's father full of pride at his beautiful daughter. John Parrish (whose many letters I have from his great-grandson, also John) described the scene to his mother: *'A Splendid Affair, everyone happy & joyful & wishing fine things for the Happy Couple. Nowhere on this day was there any sadness for anyone, that I could see. They drove away from the quay in a fine coach, horses all plumed & belled, & went from us into their new future together'.*

They lived, together and sometimes apart, at both Bristol and Brockweir. The business was still thriving, and Phillip went back into his role as *Florence's* captain, leaving his new wife during the months of that summer, and deep into the autumn. It didn't suit him. By the end of their first year, he became unhappy with his lifestyle, and longed to settle. By that time Janet was always at Brockweir, keeping the house and the few servants together. I wonder about the lack of a child – there's no mention of one in his diary, or even the probability of one, and they would surely have wanted children. We'll never know. That diary is neglected for almost all of that year – disconnected jottings, short reflections on his life, a few to-do lists, and a hasty and resolved scribble as a last entry. That slim, meagre diary ends there, on 12th December 1826 with, *'I am leaving the Sea'.* I have nothing else written by him from then on, apart from one letter to my great-great-grandmother years later.

And now there is tragedy. Later the following year, in September, Phillip was returning from Kingston, Jamaica, close to the place that had shocked him as a teenager, a place he'd never wanted to visit again. It was a voyage of convenience, as he'd taken softwood from Newfoundland into Kingston – needed for construction – and then headed back across the Atlantic with the rest of his cargo. He was to return to despair, as his Janet was dead.

∴ ∴

When *Florence* was hauled in to Bristol, Phillip was met by his friend John Parrish, who was to give him the terrible news from Brockweir. Janet had drowned in the Wye, returning from a friend in the village; the boat she shared with the boatman and his boy had overturned in the racing, flooding river. All three were gone, her body being pulled from the mud at low tide, four miles below Tintern. Phillip always thought she was a good swimmer, and apparently that's the first thing he'd said to John, in a state of shock.

He went straight away to *Casa Blanca,* to his grieving mother, and again John Parrish carried the burden of the business alone, this time allowing him his grief, rather than his joy. The next day, leaving soon after dawn, Phillip went to the churchyard of St Michael's, on the riverbank at Tintern Parva where Janet's three-week-old grave was, covered with late-summer violets and honeysuckle. John tells us that he went alone, going late in the evening to *Lower Carreg,* his sad house now empty apart from a caretaker, and stayed there for two days before returning to Bristol. It's hard to imagine his despair, which must have been extreme when the Vicar at St Michael's handed him the silver necklace, taken from Janet before burial. She'd died with it around her neck, and Phillip was to tell John sorrowfully that it should have stayed with her.

But somehow over the months that followed he was to pull himself up, and apply himself again to his work; *'He made a fool of his pain,'* wrote John, *'& became an example to all, of grief overcome, & of sadness lived with, alongside duty. He would not be cast down'.* His casting-down was to come later however, and last for many years.

It's safe to say that Phillip Rossetti was planning to leave the sea and to settle down at Brockweir, had things gone differently. He opened his heart to John Parrish, who then shared some of Phillip's hopes with his mother. John's wife Eleanor – always praised by those who knew her – would have been a source of strength to both men but I only know her husband's thoughts, through his letters to his mother at Gloucester.

Phillip had plans to turn *Lower Carreg* into an inn, but Janet had known nothing of them – the idea was to be a surprise, and now he was to go ahead with those plans without her, to carry out his dream for them both. So in the months following his tragedy, Phillip again arranged for builders at *Lower Carreg*. George Watkins, now also very alone, was pleased to be involved.

To go back to Phillip's return voyage: apart from the timber, he also brought back from Jamaica a very special thing, again, it seems, a gift for Janet – a misplaced African Grey parrot, a glorious bird, a fine grey and red *Psittacus Erithacus* in the prime of his tethered life, and an excellent mimic. This was *Aku*, his name simply meaning *parrot* among the Hausa people of West Africa. Aku was to stay with him and be his almost-constant companion, confidant and friend. He sailed the world with *Florence*, spent much time at Brockweir, and was to outlive his Master by many years. He was also to be the inspiration for the new Inn's poignant name: *The Wondrous Gift*.

## 8

## DIVIDING HIS TIME

Anna, Phillip's mother, was the calm but firm type and got on well with John Parrish – *Mrs Rossetti* familiarised to *Anna* during these years, at least in his office on the quay. She was always interested, always vigilant, and in the hard and sad times after Janet's death they would lift each other's spirits, as well as support Phillip. She kept an eye on things, as her poor husband had asked her to on his deathbed, and was seen as an asset to the business. She lasted two years from then, and when she died her beloved *Casa Blanca* in Queens Parade was given to John Parrish by a grateful Phillip. He took a few small treasured things to Brockweir, to the Inn where a landlord and his wife looked after the running of the place, and spread them around his upstairs rooms overlooking the coach road and the river. What was left in Queens Parade was given to John, his wife, and his two girls, their small garden still shared by the descendants of Captain Calvet's Genoese crocuses, many years after their long journey from Italy.

In the years after Janet's death the business settled, becoming a steady and dependable rock for Phillip, calmer than the wild decade that had ended in 1825. Now, in early 1832, and after the loss of his mother some years before, he was again feeling the hunger he'd felt before he'd met Janet. He was still grieving for her, still missing her, and restless for the family life taken from him. He spoke to John about it, as he had years before, and was apparently resigned to spending all the days left to him in a sort of troubled loneliness, and at a loss as to how to overcome it. His mother was gone, he was in his forty-fourth year and now there was a real danger of him becoming *un vecchio gentiluomo*, as she had warned. John pondered the problem, and simply stated the obvious: get out from under the weight of whatever you're carrying, and meet people. It was too simple. And Phillip had taken the huge step of finding a suitable captain for *Florence*, to take his place temporarily during the times he felt unable to take her across the world as he'd done for so long. Henry Parry, *Pensive's* captain, was the chosen one – the only one in the running, apparently. Captain Parry was truly a man of his own ilk, and between them they found a temporary captain for *Pensive*; both these captains chopped and changed their ships according to the whims and availability of Captain Phillip Rossetti – an unusual and generous agreement, and a sure measure of the respect they had for him.

Phillip was dividing his time between Bristol and Brockweir, and seemingly was in danger of becoming withdrawn while at the Inn, walking the floor of his room, staring out at the river below the bare hill opposite. The Inn itself functioned well. The bridge upriver at Bigsweir had opened in 1828, cutting out the hard road up from Monmouth and down through Whitebrook, and the resulting increase in trade was a boost to his fortunes. His landlord (of whom we know little) appears to have been efficient and amicable, along with his wife, but we do know that they were concerned for their employer. *'He keeps too much to himself,'* wrote John, *'Everyone sees it, & we feel his sadness as we feel our own.'*

Those long periods when Phillip stayed at Brockweir were worrying times for John Parrish and others at Bristol.

He came back to the Port only to be sure that things were working as they should; he walked on *Florence's* deck, but left her with Captain Parry for almost two years. He came back at odd times, and each time only for a matter of days, staying at the otherwise empty house in Charlotte Street. He appeared to be on a plateau of indifference to most things around and about, and kept company only with the parrot Aku, who went everywhere with him.

These moods were changeable though, and he could pull himself out of them sometimes, enough to focus and make decisions. It seems that a challenge, or an event out of the ordinary, could bring him back –  which helped John enormously, and suggested a real solution to Phillip's problems: keep him interested, keep him occupied. Possible at the office, but not when he took himself back to the seat of his troubles, at Brockweir. As an example, on the twelfth of March 1833 he apparently left John in a lighter mood, lifted in spirit –  after being inspired by an account of wonders to come: a direct rail connection from Bristol to London. (And it was around that time that a young Isambard Kingdom Brunel set out on horseback from Bristol with his maps, to decide the route of what he would call his Great Western Railway.) The whole idea consumed Phillip for a while, taking his mind away from his un-happiness; also, a couple of years later, and in an even more unhappy time, he'd walked up through Clifton to where the new suspension bridge was starting, and told John excitedly that he'd actually met Brunel. He'd somehow found the will to make that effort, to lose himself briefly in the excitement of the new and the daring, in the midst of his wretchedness (to think that Phillip Rossetti was there at the very beginning of my beautiful bridge is both thrilling and poignant, given his state of mind. I wish he'd been happier). John Parrish was careful to supply the right level of stimulation to Phillip, hoping to cheer him up but not transport him too far away from the things he needed to address at the office on the Mardyke Wharf. It seems he was successful enough with this, and they continued the finely-balanced process through those years, but – if only he could keep him away from Brockweir!

: : :

Now, to return to that wily bird Phillip had brought home for Janet, the Wondrous Gift whose handsome image was painted on the signboard of the Inn: he was indeed a special creature, clever, quick and loyal – but only to his master, it seems. In return Phillip doted on him, making him his own child, teaching him, and scolding when necessary. Aku learned quickly, and became known far and wide as *The Bird*. He was famous in all the villages around, in Tintern and Llandogo, in Whitebrook, down to St. Arvans, and across the river from St Briavels to Hewelsfield, up to Redbrook and beyond. The reason for this celebrity status was his talking, and it was almost his downfall.

Phillip kept him in his bedroom at the front of the Inn, and as the bird's vocabulary grew, so more and more visitors asked to see him and hear him talk, and in time this proved too much for his master. The novelty had left Phillip, and the time soon came when he refused to bring him down the dark staircase to the ground floor. People were by all accounts upset, some demanding to see the wondrous creature, especially after travelling so far... Phillip eventually refused to bring him down at all when asked, but still took him outside every evening for a period of freedom (this freedom happened first by accident, then by design, after the bird happily came back to him). In 1834 the *Monmouthshire Merlin* carried a first-hand account of a meeting with Aku, headed "The Wonderful Bird of Brockweir" which served only to increase the curiosity of many and the annoyance of Phillip. It reported the bird's vocabulary, but also the evening ritual of allowing him to fly freely around for ten minutes or so, until called back by Phillip. Aku would fly through the trees on the riverside and high up the bank above the Inn, and the only voice he would return to was his master's, and then only if a very shabby but particular broom was held up for him to land on. No broom, no Aku. His loyalty therefore became very dependant on this worn-out perch.

So to keep this business advantage while saving his reason, Phillip simply transferred the manic curiosity to another parrot. He arranged for a duplicate to be brought home some months later – another Aku, another talker, and taught him the way he'd taught the first one. He put up with everything until this new bird arrived, named him Henry, after *Pensive's* agreeable captain, and installed him downstairs in a very safe fixed cage where everyone could see him, while keeping his beloved Aku upstairs at all times, letting him in and out of his window. Henry was given less freedom, but was still allowed to fly, especially after the landlord took a shine to him and produced his very own broom in the hope of making another celebrity. The scheme worked, and visitors knew not which bird they saw, so Henry shuffled into the spotlight and left Aku to the devotions of his master.

But Phillip's sadness continued, although he took *Florence* again across to Canada that same year that Henry had arrived, the seventh year since Janet's death. It was plain that his days as a captain were running down, and we know he discussed, with John, finding a permanent Master for his favourite ship. All of this turmoil was recounted by John to his mother; he somehow stayed positive and vowed to keep everything going for his good friend, his employer. And this was the value of John Parrish, unpraised by those who came later, eclipsed by their admiration for their hero Phillip Rossetti who was barely managing his business through those years.

Everyone who knew him must have longed for a return to the old Phillip, the energetic Captain and good-humoured friend they remembered, but it seemed he would not come back to them without finding what he needed. Then, on a mild October day in 1836, he crossed the Wye to visit his friend John Easton at his boatyard along the bank. There were other visitors for John Easton that day: Edward Price, and his daughter Catherine, from Hereford. They knew the Easton family, and had called in en route to Chepstow. Catherine was thirty-four, an almost-resigned spinster, another poor soul under the threat of a life lived alone. Phillip explained to John Parrish in some detail of how he met Catherine at the boatyard and was again hit with the feeling of *she is the one for me*. Catherine was gracious, and took well to him, while her father observed, and wondered.

They were Catholics, and so was Phillip; all that would be needed was for him to un-lapse himself and to take Mass, to involve himself in what Catherine's family did. He was surprisingly prepared to do those things to win her, and when she realised quite soon that he was serious, she made her feelings known and life again looked up for Phillip

Rossetti. After their brief first meeting she'd continued with her father to Chepstow, but stayed for two days at the Inn on their return. Everyone breathed a sigh of relief for a life – *two lives* – hopefully saved from loneliness.

So another happy period began for Phillip as a month later he and Catherine were betrothed in Hereford, and planned to marry the following September. It was around this time that he firmly decided to give up his seafaring life, which had anyway become very irregular; a new captain wasn't necessary, as he would take *Florence* to the end of her working life himself, and they would retire from the sea together. His faithful ship was then fifty-seven years old, and showing her age; she was always looked after well, but in spite of a few restorations in recent years it was no longer wise to load her fully. *Florence's* days were almost over, and the business would continue with *Pensive*, *Anna Elena* and *Montclair*. John Parrish says that she left the harbour for the last time on the first of May in the year of Phillip's marriage, was towed across to Newport to an undecided future, and that her steadfast Captain was remarkably composed – looking upon it as a timely end for *Florence* and a new start for himself. He'd captained her for the last time to Riga, a shorter trip than she was used to, and brought her back into Bristol with flags and pennants flying. A month after that he and John watched a steam tug take her from the harbour, filled with ballast instead of cargo, through the lock and away, Phillip with Aku gripped on his arm. Those three were surely sad for their old friend, but the times felt hopeful: it was the end of an era, and the start of another.

## 9

YOUR LOVING & DEVOTED PHILLIP

Preparations were underway for Phillip's second wedding. There were several day-long trips to Hereford for him, and he also took Catherine to Bristol; her mother went with them and was in charge of almost everything, according to John, whose own mother was acutely interested in their goings-on.

Janet's silver necklace had meanwhile lain in Phillip's desk drawer at the Inn, a ten-year rest during which I imagine its keeper often lifted and held it close –  but I know I imagine too much of him. It is true though that he wanted Catherine to wear it at their marriage, but he would have known how difficult this would be for her, so he wrote on the fifth of August 1837 to her father's house in Hereford. This single, hopeful letter is all we have from Phillip Rossetti during those years:

> *"My Beloved Catherine,*
> *I write from Bristol, where I am kept these three weeks,*
> *& trust that You are Well & that Your Family will be*
> *mindful of Your Needs until My return. The days are*
> *long & tiresome without You, & My Heart is Tender &*
> *looks ahead to Our Meeting again.*
> *I have a request to put before You, which I am hoping*
> *You will find agreeable. It concerns the Silver Pendant*
> *& Chain which was as You know given to Janet on our*
> *Wedding Day & which was saved from the River. As it*
> *escaped Her Fate, I wish it to continue its Journey.*
> *I am not superstitious. I want You to share its Love &*

*its Beauty, & pass it on for as long as we have Rossetti Brides. I wish You to allow Them all to do that. If this offends You, please take time to consider, but remove superstition from Your judgement. There is no evil nor ill intent in this Necklace, indeed there is an Abundance of Love contained within it which is directed at You. It was made for My Bride, & You are to be Her. It has no remembrance of its past & if We Ourselves remember then it should be with thankfulness for its true intentions & Hope for its promised future. I beg You to consider this request, and to look favourably upon it.*

*I will return in good time at the end of August, all being well. Please give my Best Regards to Your Father & Mother.*

*I am Your Loving & Devoted*
*Phillip."*

His hope was not to be realised, as Catherine refused to wear jewellery made for another wife – and especially, given its history, taken from a *dead* wife. My grandmother Georgina told me as much and said she herself had no such fears, and was the second Rossetti bride, fifty-four years after Janet, to wear the necklace. If only Phillip could have known this, his disappointment with Catherine may have been comforted.

They married in the first year of the Victorian era, in September 1837, at the then hidden-away Catholic Church of St Mary, in Monmouth. He was forty-nine, she thirty-five – respectable ages, and to those who knew of their wish for children there must have been an aura of *leaving it a bit late.* After the ceremony they left for Brockweir with the intention of setting up home, with Phillip away on occasional short trips to Bristol. They would go together on longer trips, and stay at Charlotte Street; this was a new way forward for him, a promise to himself that wife and family would be part of his life and not left far away for long. He would never lose his profound regret at not having had more time with Janet.

So their lives together began, with Catherine taking on the management of *The Wondrous Gift*. We don't know what she thought of the Inn's name, but she surely needed some understanding of Phillip's loss ten years before, and to be able to accept her situation in surroundings that were all contrived for Janet. They travelled the eight miles to Monmouth every Sunday for Mass, and once a month for Confession. Phillip drove her in the carriage, in all weathers, the level roads being easy even in the winter snows.

At Brockweir there were a few early problems '*concerning the Duties of the two Ladies present, the Landlord's Wife & the new Lady of the House*,' wrote John, whose mother had foreseen certain difficulties in the hierarchy. They were ironed out, it seems, and Phillip was no doubt able to sit at his desk without the distraction of an unhappy Catherine. Aku shared their lives, observed, and learned new words, while Phillip wished he could forget some others he'd picked up during his early time at Kingston – namely a few basic obscenities in Spanish, which luckily were lost on his new wife... she was easier to offend than Janet would have been.

They lived on the first floor, in Phillip's rooms, and took up all the front of the Inn, which left space for seven more guest rooms of various sizes behind them. Their access was private, with their own staircase, and the layout is the same to this day – a self-contained suite of rooms where my granddaughter Alice now lives with her husband Jon. I'm sorry I never lived there, the beloved home of Phillip Rossetti, but my life was far away in Bristol.

Sometimes these days, when it's sunny, I drive to Brockweir and park in front of *The Wondrous Gift*. My daughter Elena is somewhere inside, and Alice, and there is movement behind the windows facing me – unknown people going about their business. The hill rises at the back, steep to the top, and trees overhang the patch of garden and the winding paths to right and left. This is the place I'm writing about – Phillip's doomed wish for Janet, his refuge during his lonely years, and later his family home. It looks across to Brockweir village, still with the old buildings but long since closed down from industry and unrest, the village now quiet and welcoming, the newer houses spreading along the bank across from the hotel.

The river continues, the only unchangeable part of the scene, not needing to grow, to be updated, or modernised. It's the same as Phillip would have seen it, and Janet, and Catherine, and all the others. I can get lost in this; I have no need to work, beyond a little painting or cutting some grass, and my days could easily be empty and free. So now and then I come back to what has become the centre of my past, more so than Bristol, or London – this feels like my home, though I never lived here. I dream too much of Brockweir, but also of Bristol, where it's hard to imagine life all those years ago, long before my time, but that's where I came from; those people were my ancestors, some good, some less so, and I'm pleased that one of the good ones came here, and built this place.

: : :

From what I can gather Phillip and Catherine were happy with each other, and there's not much to suggest that Phillip became aware of anything to detract from the *pure and perfect love* he spoke to John about before his marriage. But I know that Phillip Rossetti – ever the idealist, though without doubt not perfect himself – was not able to forget his first love; she would become more perfect as time passed... and unfair competition for Catherine. John wrote (again to his mother, his faraway confidant): *'Phillip has said to me on occasion of how he feels close still with Janet & wishes it were not so, as her memory is a large presence in his household. He is unable to change his fond remembrances of her, nor in truth does he wish to, but HOPES her memories will diminish, as he all the while allows them to flourish.'*

We don't know the effect this stubborn devotion had on Catherine, but she must have been indulgent to the man she loved, and hopeful of eventually replacing Janet in his thoughts. As for pure and perfect love, I'm not convinced... if it existed, it was surely for his untainted memory of Janet rather than Catherine. But overall they were happy, by all accounts.

John Parrish was now in charge of the entire Bristol operation, and settled into the routine of regular visits from Phillip. *Pensive, Anna Elena* and *Montclair* were kept busy and there's not much to report beyond the reality of a successful business. John's daughters were now grown up; the eldest, Helen, was married and lived south of the city at Whitchurch, and the other, twenty-year-old Elizabeth, lived at home and worked with him in his office on the quay. Phillip's input was dealing with the many non-urgent requests from John, his Captains, his agents and others in the Port regarding everything from minor gripes to maintenance schedules and faraway reports from the great forests of the world... he would carry all this paperwork home with him, and it would be resolved by his next visit. He was one of the early homeworkers, but always kept his finger firmly on the Bristol pulse – he had definitely not retired.

At the end of October he'd announced to John that Catherine was pregnant – a child was coming, who if timely would arrive in the month of June, into the sunshine and warmth. John says he'd never seen him happier (but he had, I think) and he returned to Brockweir, after his regular day at the office, in excellent spirits. Catherine was well, and he began his closer-than-usual duty of care, as his father Pietro had done with Phillip's mother.

The months went by uneventfully, and as the last one approached he took no risks, installing a midwife in one of the guest rooms, and putting the local doctor at Tintern on short notice. When it happened though, there was no fuss, and the doctor arrived an hour after the event, the midwife being sufficient. Catherine and Phillip Rossetti had a new daughter.

Whether he'd especially wanted a son or not, I have no idea, but I feel it mattered less to him that she was a girl – his seafaring days were over, and I don't think he would have been so anxious for a new captain to follow him. He was very happy with his daughter, and he would name her Phillipa Anna Elena, after himself and his mother –  I suspect Catherine had no say in the names. Baby Phillipa would be cared for mostly by a painstakingly-chosen nurse, as was the fashion for wealthy families, and during the months ahead be paraded through the villages and in Monmouth, but never across to Brockweir, even though life was safer there in those days. Phillip had forbidden his wife and child to ever be ferried across, or even to go close to the river; the hardened, un-superstitious sea-captain still suffered with the memory of his first love, and must have feared this small span of water. The ferry, however, was well used. A church had been founded in 1833 by the Moravians, after the Duke of Beaufort petitioned for Christian morals in Brockweir. It was eagerly built on one of the cockfighting pits, and many people came to the services from both sides of the Wye. The village appeared to be stabilised at last, but it's safe to say that baby Phillipa never went there while her father was alive. The river trade was busier than ever, and bigger shipyards along the bank turned out brigs and schooners – big ships to go far beyond the Wye. Over the years a few chapels would be built, and a school, and this, coupled with a new railway and the slow running down of its old trade, was to forever change the character of the village by the early nineteen-hundreds.

10

## LITTLE PHILLIPA

Little Phillipa Rossetti: what can I say about this beautiful child that will soften my feelings towards her as she grew up? Nothing, I fear, and one hundred and sixty years later I can give that innocent baby no more than ordinary love, while thinking back to her father – my favourite ancestor, you remember – because seemingly all he stood for was to be turned on its head and spoiled by this creature, then so lovely and new, unsullied and open to everything.  She would be my father's grandmother... his evil inspiration and my long-dead burden, and far worse than he would ever be. She is the main demon in this story, the tyrant who taught my father, and in turn both of these people developed the business I would one day turn away from.
So how do children turn into demons?

We easily blame their parents, the ones who influence them, the ones who prepare their ground. What I know of Catherine is scant – a kind, almost-fervent Catholic, without doubt spoiled by her parents, and someone not used to hardship of any sort. That's very broad. Philip, I know more of – a disillusioned Catholic (outwardly brought back some-what by Catherine), not spoiled, used to hard physical and mental work, and a man with principles. Broad pictures, leaving out all the shades of character also in the mix. People are complex. The fact remains though that Phillipa the baby, became – twenty-one years later – Phillipa the owner of the Rossetti business, and from then on that business flourished largely because of her greed and callousness. She was to know her father for just one year, and through her life she would be uninterested in his principles, and ignore them all; one year was not enough, and the spoiled mother would go on to spoil the child in spectacular fashion.

Phillip had died ten days after his daughter's first birthday. The simple act of walking through a summer storm apparently brought on pneumonia, and he died some days later in the sunlit bedroom at the front of the Inn. John Parrish came from Bristol, arriving too late to speak to his friend, and stayed as long as he could to console Catherine, who was in despair. She was now the owner of the entire business, the Inn, and the house in Charlotte Street, and, understandably at that point, '*...quite unable to gather her thoughts in any sensible order, with regard to her future as owner of such an Enterprise.*'

John left her the next day in the care of the landlord and his wife until her mother could come from Hereford, and returned to Bristol, to an even greater workload than before.

Catherine's family worshipped at St Francis Xavier, in Hereford, but there was no Catholic cemetery there, so Phillip was buried a week later at St Michael's, in Abergavenny, which is possibly not what he would have chosen for himself. Beyond Janet, I'm guessing he would have wanted to be with his parents in Bristol, but Catherine's mind was set, or she had no say in the matter – probably both. It may have cheered him had he known that the same Archangel would watch over him there as watched over his first wife at the little church of St Michael in Tintern.

: : :

When a child loses a father, the mother has a stark and fateful responsibility. She is largely answerable for how the child develops, and after losing her husband, Catherine, it seems, simply lost her wits over Phillipa. She despaired, not knowing how to proceed, and in doing so gave their daughter everything. She was wealthy, and it appears the only way she knew to make up to the child for her loss was to shower her with gifts, with whatever the child desired. It was easy, and would have the predictable effect of turning the little girl into an uncaring and self-centred bully, intent on getting her own way with everyone. She was bright, and would soon learn the fruitful arts of manipulation.

When John returned to Brockweir two weeks after Phillip's death, little Phillipa charmed him with her curiosity, and the endearing way she baby-talked with Aku, Phillip's grief-stricken soulmate. The wondrous bird was not eating and had gone into what would become a month-long silence, only to come out after Catherine asked the landlord for help. Henry was brought up, to be told abruptly by Aku (my father writes) to *bugger off*; this encounter however brought him out of his stupor and he resumed his mutterings, albeit more low-key than before. John says the landlord helped Catherine with the broom routine, as she wanted to replace her husband in the bird's favours; she held out the broom and after a worrying start, for fear of him not ever coming back, Aku honoured her by returning to it. He'd lived with Phillip for fourteen years, and would outlive Catherine herself – I would dearly love to hear what he witnessed in his lifetime.

In that summer of 1839, John Parrish had many problems. He had sleepless nights worrying over his new employer, who couldn't face her position and could never be a replacement for Phillip. Over the next month she began to show interest, but John's mother had to be deterred from coming down to Bristol, wanting to help him. A letter dated August 28th puts us in the picture: '*...the Business continues here, & important & necessary actions are taken. My wages are paid, & those of my men are ready for their return. My new Employer is all the while recovering from her ordeal & I am certain that she will soon take up her proper position as Head of the Company. She has visited here this past week & shows great promise. I am sure that all will be well.*'

He needed to calm his mother, but John was also being honest, it seems. Catherine *was* showing promise, staying several times at Charlotte Street with her mother and Phillipa, and slowly going through the unfamiliar duties. She apparently had no intention of moving to Bristol, and after the huge effort of overcoming her loss went back to running the Inn, where her mother had brought Catherine's younger cousin Rhiannon from Abergavenny to help her.

She told John she would rely on him to run the business, allowing him to take on more help for his daughter in the office, and raising his wages, and even with all his doubts he carried on. He took on an under-manager, but felt that he'd somehow become Phillip in all but name and wealth. He wrote about how fragile he felt to be doing things his employer used to do, taking decisions which would never have been his to make while Phillip were alive. There was no one above him to even share his responsibilities. He carried on, it seems, out of a sense of duty to his old friend, and to Catherine and the child. He was paid well, but I think not well enough for his position. He had the house in Queens Parade and a job many envied, but he worried about his future, about becoming old and taking the strain, and of supporting his wife and himself if he were ever to lose his job. He'd never once dreamed of being where he now was.

Catherine could not take her husband's place, but over her first years of widowhood she became more helpful. She came every month with Phillipa to Bristol and sat in the office with John, discussing anything he raised with her, but from his letters it appears that this amounted to not much; he says she was always interested and encouraging, but as for policy decisions or just plain understanding, she was lacking. Her girl was growing up and already showing the behaviour that would later cause her despair, and this consumed her. John thought the child was far more important to her than the business, but stopped short of saying so, contenting himself with the fact that she visited him regularly. Nevertheless it was a poor recipe for continued success. He felt he would eventually lose Catherine altogether, with unknown consequences. The girl, he knew, would take all her life and spirit, and the behaviour he saw during their visits filled him with dread – she could possibly be his future employer, but at fifty-four he thought it unlikely he'd live to see that day.

∴ ∴ ∴

Catherine's life without Phillip was barren, even with her cousin smoothing her way. Rhiannon was ten years younger and more used to hard work; she settled in to one of the guest rooms, quietly doing what she could but not being able to break into Catherine's solitude. Phillip was gone after five short years, and she was now more lonely than before their meeting, before the days when she'd thought there was no one in the world for her. In her fortieth year she was to close in on herself and seek privacy, even though she was now a far more desirable catch – wealthy, in good health and still with the soft beauty that had caught Phillip. There would be no shortage of suitors if she wanted them, but I can imagine her needing to be alone yet hating that particular loneliness, especially at the busy Inn.

She lived with her daughter, the strange toddler who would not obey, who would not try to be pleasant unless it suited her, and she must have wept inwardly and prayed for a miraculous change of heart to bring Phillipa towards her. She soon needed to think of her schooling, but came up against the same block that Phillip's parents had met when they came to Bristol – there were no Catholic schools anywhere near. The nearest was in Hereford, but she refused her parents' offer to board the child with them. Intent on bringing up Phillipa in her sight, Catherine was not doing a good job with her and she knew it, but she soldiered on in a fog of incompetence. No boundaries were ever set firmly enough and the child was able to climb over everything in her way, building confidence as she went, and as she grew she never felt under any obligation to tell the truth about anything, unless that truth would help her. Too bad to be true, almost.

Catherine deserves compassion for her hopes, but things were obviously badly awry by the time a private tutor was brought in, when Phillipa was four. She would be taught in her father's study for the next fifteen years, by a Catholic governess, and apparently fought hard against the rigours of the largely religious regime. She would forever complain bitterly of the harshness of her education – and could never understand the connection between education and religion. She would later thoroughly denounce Catholicism, and refuse to allow it (or any other faith) to touch her daughter Georgina. So our family, in one generation, lost its Catholic base, and Georgina would much later tell me that she waited in an uncomfortable spiritual wilderness until she joined the Church of England at twenty-three, some years after leaving her mother.

Catherine slowly came out of her despair, and ran the Inn with her cousin, now permanent, and along with the landlord and his wife the business was easily managed. Seasons and travellers came, lingered, and moved on. She tried, with the Governess, to keep little Phillipa within the Catholic fold, but the child's sincerity was lacking – even with the pretty candles and tinkling bells of the morning Mass. John tells us she became so difficult and abusive that the Governess almost left: '*...these are hard times at Brockweir. Mrs Rossetti is at her wits end with her daughter & I greatly fear how the child will grow. Her Governess is too mild for everyones liking & joins too much with Mrs Rossetti rather than standing on her own. We look from Bristol & wonder how long these affairs can continue. The latest news is that the Governess is to move out & we hope that if that happens then a stronger teacher can be found. To be so ruled by a six-years child is a position that should not be endured.*'

But the six years' child *did* rule.

Her schoolwork she usually found easy, but as the years passed she wore her teacher down with her reluctance to take on any religious duties. The morning Mass, always held in her mother's bedroom, became a time of anxiety. The mysterious devotions left her cold, and by the time Phillipa was ten neither mother nor Governess could persuade her to happily take part in anything faith-based.

John was perplexed: '*The notion of God has filled her with dread, not fear, & she fights with His very existence. We can do nothing but wonder at where this dislike springs from.*' But being wilful she just took the route that pleased her most.

John Parrish feared for his future.

## 11

## JOHN PARRISH

Phillipa's growing-up could be a book in itself, but she's having one chapter for it, which begins in 1848 when she was ten. By that time her mother had long given up on her becoming the daughter she'd wished for, and the Governess – her third – had also given in, especially in matters of religion. The child screamed her way out of any situation she didn't like, and only consented to study subjects she found easy – mainly mathematics and book-keeping. Languages were out, literature was out, anything remotely female was out. Catherine's dream of a quiet child, content with embroidery, music or reading French prose, remained a dream.

John Parrish stayed in Bristol, quite hostile to any thoughts of visiting Brockweir. Now sixty years old, his fears over his future were acute, and though the Business thrived he couldn't help thinking ahead to this impossible child becoming mature and actually being his employer. He prayed hopefully each night for Catherine's health, and wrote often to his now-ancient mother for encourage-ment. '*You must be strong,*' she wrote back, '*& You must think of giving up that Profession. Save your money & be frugal with life, for I think she will let you go when her Mother passes. Heed me, & see what a dissolute she is. She will have no pity. She will dominate you or destroy you, & either is to be avoided.*'

He knew all that. He also knew how helpless Catherine was, and how the Business would unravel if he left.

Catherine kept up her monthly visits to Bristol. She always travelled with Phillipa, and the pair of them sat in John's office while he went over anything that needed to be discussed. During one of these meetings, the ten-year-old said something that shook him and brought Catherine to tears. One precious – and crucial – letter to his mother says it all: *'The child, after hearing the month's returns, questions the wisdom of trading in timber. Her manner was loud and noxious as ever. She (at ten years) wishes us to trade in sugar and tobacco, for the profit of the Business. She demands to know why this is not done. Understand me, she demands to know. Her poor mother broke into tears & my explanations regarding the sanctity of her father's wishes & the decision taken by him and myself regarding this Trade those many years ago, she swept aside. I very much think that your heartfelt words will become the truth & I will be overlooked if ever her mother allows her any say in these affairs.'*

This was a calamity.

Catherine, who by now fully realised that her own weakness was the reason for her daughter's behaviour but was not able to move her at all, sank deeper into despair. She knew the older the child became the stronger she would be, and long before her coming-of-age the pressure could become irresistible from her. She spoke privately to John and assured him that while she was alive Phillipa would not have her way, but he doubted her, and prepared to think hard about his future. He would have a pension from the Business, of course... so it appears he wanted to hang on for the sake of his old friend Phillip, at least until the girl was of an age to take over properly, when John could leave her to it. He should not have had any great money worries in his retirement.

I read his letters now with great sadness. He thought he would have six or seven years before his time was up, yet he knew that Phillipa would not have the trust of any merchant – and therefore could not run the Business – before she was twenty-one, and even then it would be extraordinary for such a young woman to be in charge of an enterprise this complex. But – '*My fear increases & my thoughts spring from one possibility to another, each worse than its predecessor. It is most likely that the girl will wear down that good Lady & I will be told to follow her proposals, under her mother's guidance. This I feel will happen long before her majority comes. So I prepare to be ruled by my employer Mrs Rossetti, who will speak the words of her daughter, yet equally I prepare to be cast out before that will happen.*'

Six or seven years: he would be an old man, looking to retire anyway, but he would go on to fight for "the Sanctity of Her Father's wishes". He carried on as before, the three ships busy as ever, the profits steady, and on his employer's subsequent visits he remained calm and steadfast in his opinions of the right thing to do. He even agreed with Phillipa that more money was to be made her way, but told her every time that it was impossible while he was in charge – thus digging his own grave. She ranted, always demanding to know why he would turn down greater profits, and he always gave her the same answer: because of your father, and my own conscience. Every month was the same – her way was the best and only way. John stood up to her, dreading her visits but calmly resisting… and this went on for eight interminable years, a year more than he'd thought, a hundred visits and a hundred unbalanced arguments, with Catherine visibly shrinking into the submission he knew would come; it came in 1856 – he was sixty-eight, his nemesis was eighteen

: : :

John Parrish's mother died in that same year, a short while before her son was ousted by Phillipa. It was bittersweet for him – sadness, and gratitude for her not seeing his humiliation. Her last letter to him says, *"I trust that God will look over You for what You have done, & give You His Reward, which awaits all Good people. Rest in the sure knowledge that the woman you fear will receive the Judgement she deserves. Believe that, & be joyful for your decency & honesty & faithfulness to the memory of your Honourable Friend Phillip."*

She was gone, no more letters, no more encouragement.

The details I have from here on are from everywhere: from my mother Alicia, and her mother-in-law Georgina – Phillipa's daughter – shocking and sad tales passed on and likely embellished on their way. My father's *True Account* also tells of this time, but again its title is proved false; his opinion of John Parrish came from Phillipa, who by the time she'd reached eighteen, it's safe to say, despised him. So my father wrote: *'It became time for John Parrish to move aside, & to allow a Younger mind to apply itself to our Business. My Grandmother Phillipa (at Eighteen years old!) was to set a more Profitable course, previously denied Her by this wasteful, blinkered man.'*

Early on that dark November morning in 1856, Phillipa arrived at John's office alone, her mother left in dejection at Brockweir with her cousin Rhiannon, and Aku. The story goes that there was no preamble, just a cold statement of fact: John Parrish was to retire immediately, and a new Manager would replace him until she was old enough to take over herself. This was all with the permission of her mother, who would support all she'd said. Catherine came the next day, with Phillipa, and confirmed the new arrangement; a

Manager had already been found, and John was given two days to tie any loose ends, and clear his desk. *Voilà!* The girl had won, as he knew she would – it was her birthright to have the Business and there were no profound surprises, just sad confirmation.

And that should have been it. There was no need for ranting anymore. But she was Phillipa, and she was unable to let her anger go; those two days were the worst of John Parrish's life, by all accounts except my father's. He was harried by her each day – she'd moved into the house in Charlotte Street, and a housekeeper looked after most things for her (Phillipa, in her mind, had already moved Charlotte Street five hundred yards up the hill, out of Brandon and into Clifton, a better address for her. She chose to call it Charlotte Street, Clifton – keeping the lie for the rest of her life, and sometimes being caught out. I wonder why she didn't really move, but then her atheism would have been against her in rampantly-Anglican Clifton, where everyone went to church, so she was perhaps safer beyond the fringe, and anyway she appears to have been comfortable with lies. When Pietro had bought that house in 1814, he didn't care that it was just beyond the limits of good taste, neither did Phillip, but for Phillipa, and later my father, the deception was necessary).

Poor John was unaware that she'd been at Charlotte Street, a few hundred yards up the hill in front of his own house, for several days before her visit. It was efficient, and ruthless towards a man who deserved much better – and to make matters worse, she also dismissed his daughter Elizabeth, an unnecessary act since she would not have stayed without her father, but Phillipa would have enjoyed turning her out.

John Parrish went home after that second day, and with his wife and daughter would have consoled each other over the end of Phillip Rossetti's business, the end of what we would now call his ethical business plan. Things would soon change, and he was to see his beloved ships coming in one by one over the weeks and months ahead, to be emptied of their timber and converted for sugar, tobacco, cotton and all the cargoes he'd avoided for so long.

But Phillipa was not to leave it there with John. I've looked through the company ledgers of that time, and confirmed the story that she cut his pension: two payments of the contracted amount were made, and halved from then on. He wrote – naively – to the Rossetti's solicitor on August 3rd, 1856: *'This is contrary to the Law, and must be challenged ... she throws Queens Parade at me, saying it is payment enough, but it earns me nothing & must be maintained.'* He was to fight for more than a year, without success, as she kept him at bay with legalities, hoping to wear him out. She was successful. At the start of the new year of 1858, John Parrish died; Catherine – who had avoided him the whole year before – gave some of her own money to his widow Eleanor, being forbidden to part with Company money in that direction.

Eleanor gave up the fight for John's rights, and his half-pension sustained her at Queens Parade. She lived with Elizabeth and I imagine them making the best of their lives there, reliving the good times when John and Phillip had raised the Rossetti business above the greedy customs of the day, before the influence of Phillipa took hold. I hope there were bright days for them to enjoy, days of walking the town and the hill above the house, of tending their garden, and they could spend their days in contentment for their past. I know that after Eleanor's death Elizabeth married and stayed there, in the house Phillip had given to John that looked forever across the old harbour, in full view of the Rossetti comings and goings.

## 12

## RICHARD SPARKS

In 1860, on the morning of December 20th, a body was fished out of the Float at Welsh Back and carried away on a cart to St Peter's Hospital. *The Bristol Gazette* ran the story:

> *'The unfortunate Gentleman, a Mr Richard Sparks, was the husband of Mrs Phillipa Sparks of Rossetti Shipping & Trading (of Mardyke and Clifton), of which Mr Sparks was the Owner and Manager. He appears to have fallen into the Float near the Llandoger Tavern Inn some time during the night of the 14th to the 15th last. The Landlord of the Inn, Mr C Morris, has confirmed that the deceased was seen in his establishment on the evening of the 14th, and left some time after 10 o'clock. Any pertinent information regarding this tragedy should be reported to the Constabulary at St Phillips.'*

Richard Sparks was the Manager brought in to replace John Parrish; his wife was Phillipa Rossetti. So the man pulled from the Float was the father of her daughter Georgina, and therefore my great-grandfather.

But all is not well here, because of circumstance: Put simply, the Property Law of England in 1860 states, *'The property of any woman, upon marriage, becomes the property of her husband.'* Why therefore would someone like Phillipa Rossetti marry, knowing that she'd also give up her property, her newly-acquired business and her income, to her husband, to do as he wished with? It's so unlikely to me, even though I know the Rossetti family line would have ended with her if she'd stayed single; she may have wanted a child to pass it on to... but that child would always be at her husband's mercy, not hers; and that same law also states that the only way for a married woman to regain her property, is through widowhood.

So, for the past year I admit to living too much in that winter of 1860, and to having a brazen obsession with the possibility –   actually the *probability* for me, knowing Phillipa as I think I do – of the unlawful, but convenient death of Richard Sparks.

∴ ∴ ∴

As John Parrish left, in late summer 1856, Richard Sparks entered. He was a brash man by all accounts –  even my father's – and rather too full of confidence to be likeable, but that could have been a positive trait to Phillipa and one of the reasons for taking him on. She was eighteen, strong enough to bully her mother into agreeing with her, and strong-willed enough to know exactly what she wanted. She had almost three years to wait for the total control she craved, but Richard Sparks would do her bidding in the meantime.

He was seven years older than her, and new to Bristol, having arrived from Taunton where he'd spent his days working for his father's accountancy business. Just after his twenty-fifth birthday his uncle had died and left him 'upwards of twenty thousand pounds', and he immediately left his job and his parents to spread his wings in the Capital of the West Country. She'd found him through one of John's clerks, a turncoat who'd met Richard one evening in The Nova Scotia public house at Cumberland Basin. Our *True Account* gives my father's slant on the situation: '*Richard Sparks, a capable Gentleman of twenty-five Years & of independent means, entered the Service of Rossetti Shipping & Trading, & led the way to*

*Greater Profits under the Guidance of his Employer, my Grandmother Phillipa. To know that Her age was just Eighteen Years, & to realise Her Qualities of Leadership & Management (which were to give great momentum to our Business in the years following) is to further Our Admiration of Her.'*

Good stuff, but my father *was* a little biased.

Richard Sparks was a success, however. The accounts show an abrupt change of fortune in the first six months, and he and his young muse must have felt as high as Phillip and John had when they expanded in 1815. The timber markets were all but abandoned as they switched to Jamaican sugar and molasses, joining the other merchants in their great quest for greater profit.

Those first three years were spent in rebranding the Business from timber importers to traders in West Indian and North American commodities, the high-yield cargoes, the rich fruits of slavery. My references for this time are the Company accounts and my father's history, which agree with each other more or less... he praises everything and everyone because the profits grew, and when Phillipa turned twenty-one, Rossetti Shipping & Trading was among the wealthiest businesses in the Port. She was a high-achiever, a young woman who ruled the roost in her little world of men, and I wish I could be proud of her. I have a faded sepia photograph – she's nineteen, sitting in a studio in an almost-impossible hooped crinoline – at the cutting-edge of fashion, her hair parted severely and coiled into ringlets each side of her face, the whole look perfectly Victorian. Her features are not hard though, and she stares straight at the lens, defiantly presenting herself as Phillipa Rossetti, caretaker and soon-to-be owner of Rossetti Shipping & Trading, of Clifton, Bristol.

Two years after that picture, on Phillipa's birthday, her

mother Catherine signed everything away, sitting at her husband's study window at Brockweir, having refused to do it in Bristol. Nothing would have mattered to Phillipa, as long as her mother's signature was on the documents, but she didn't get *The Wondrous Gift* – Catherine held onto those deeds, terrified of her daughter owning the roof over her head. Phillipa left for Bristol with her solicitor the same day, to return to the Inn only twice more in her lifetime.

Two months passed, then she shocked everyone by becoming betrothed to her manager. My father wrote about it of course – but many years later, when he knew the outcome – and I think had he been able to be there he would have been aghast at the thought, unaware of how things would turn out, but despairing at the possibilities. Just as well he wasn't. He concludes that they would be stronger together, a child would be needed, and with hindsight praises her decision. He later calls Richard Sparks' death a tragedy, but he was lying, as he often did.

Phillipa and Richard married at Clifton Register Office in February, to the sadness of her mother, who came over and sat in the dull room as her daughter married a man Catherine had hardly met, and didn't know. There were no celebrations – and no honeymoon to come – and Catherine went back to Brockweir to her cousin and her Aku, back to the distractions of the Inn. Phillipa took her new husband to Charlotte Street. Their daughter Georgina was born a perfect ten months later, disproving what many must have reasoned.

: : :

*The Llandoger Trow* is one of the famous inns of Bristol, sitting close to the quayside at Welsh Back, which is where the trows from the Wye would load and unload. In the mid-1800s it was *The Llandoger Tavern,* and Welsh Back was a busy wharf. By night the area was busier and more dangerous to the casual visitor. Many deaths are recorded along the Floating Harbour, usually from drunkenness, and violence from sailors getting what they could from strangers and quickly moving on. Fights and disorder were normal.

Richard Sparks was not a casual visitor. He was used to spending most of his evenings at the Inn before he'd married Phillipa, and in the manner of the time, nothing changed after their marriage. Whether she minded or not, I have no idea. Maybe she didn't. It was all part of normal life in those days, where the husband was in charge, and believed he owned his wife, like the property that became his on the day they married, by the Law of England.

I also have no idea whether Richard was a good husband... but what was a good husband in 1860? In their social circle, he would be successful (easy to measure), and generous to his wife (open to interpretation). To my annoyance, nothing has been found from their time together which tells of their relationship, so I shy away from assumptions, or worse, being creative. I have resisted.

The first information I have of Richard Sparks' death is that report from the *Bristol Gazette* the day after he was found. This was followed up the next day with a plea from the then-young Bristol Constabulary for information on another man, seen leaving the Inn moments after Richard left that night. This man was known to them:

*'The Inspector requests that anyone with information as to the whereabouts of Thomas Grant, a sailor, formerly an employee of Rossetti Shipping & Trading, should*

*inform him at the earliest opportunity at the Constabulary in St Phillips. This man was seen leaving the Llandoger Tavern shortly after Mr Sparks on the night of the 14th, and may have information which would help the Investigation.'*

An alibi for Richard's death thus appears: Thomas Grant was dismissed for petty theft two days before the 14th, and could have had a grudge against the man who dismissed him – Richard Sparks. The crew records state that he was caught stealing on board *Montclair,* and later discharged without pay (a note is written in pencil against the entry – "A very bad man" – no doubt left there by an unhappy clerk after the loss of his Master).

So far, so good.

My thoughts about Phillipa's involvement are not all from my dislike of her (though that doesn't help), but from the known circumstances. My darkest thoughts are that she had a healthy child, and therefore Richard Sparks had fulfilled his duty to her, and could be removed; if he died, she would have her freedom, his money, and their child. Four weeks after the birth, Thomas Grant gave her the opportunity she needed, and two days after that, Richard was dead. She would see an advantage in the sailor's bitterness, approach him and offer him money for the task... half now, half when it's done – as always, a prudent plan. This would be fanciful, except for the fact that Thomas Grant was himself pulled from the Float two days after Richard was, but at the Mardyke, and with a pistol ball lodged in his brain. And two items went missing: a pair of Deringer pistols belonging to Richard, and kept locked up in his office – pistols of the same calibre as the shot that killed Thomas Grant.

My greatest finds were the original Police reports of the two deaths, and of the investigation. Newspapers, then as now, looked for the sensational and there are a few stories which safely fall into the creative slot with their dubious 'eye-witness accounts' of the events, which have little similarity to the Police record.

It was known that Richard Sparks owned those two pistols. They were shown to visitors, and much admired; he'd bought them from an American captain, and kept them in his office in their Walnut case. The Police Inspector asked to see them after Thomas Grant's death, no doubt following a thread of his own regarding reasons and alibis, and noted that

> *'Mrs Sparks was forthcoming in the explanation that her husband had taken them both with him on the night he died, she not knowing the reason why, but suggested that Mr Sparks was perhaps intending to show them off at the Tavern.'*

This is odd – she would surely have asked him why. It was not normal for gentlemen to be armed, apart from a sturdy cane perhaps, so why did he take them, if in fact he did? To impress someone, to harm someone, or to protect himself? They would presumably have been in his pockets, and either were lost in the water, or were taken from him before he went in. And what of Thomas Grant?

> *'A ball was taken away from the pistol case, and found to be of similar gauge to the one taken from the deceased, Mr Grant. This is not conclusive, but requires further examination.'*

Phillipa was actually taken to the Constabulary for questioning; if she were guilty, she would have seen that coming, and if innocent, I imagine her being genuinely outraged. According to the report, she was calm:

> *'When questioned over the missing pistols, she repeated her previous explanation, while showing no signs of obvious distress apart from grief at her recent loss. The Inspector asked why, if it could be assumed that Mr Sparks had taken the pistols to show them off, he had not taken them in their handsome case, with the powder, spare balls and priming flask, which would surely show them to their best advantage, to which Mrs Sparks had no answer.'*

She was asked about her movements on the night before Thomas Grant was found, and admitted to leaving her house at nine-thirty to fetch something from the office on the quayside. As it was not wise for any lady to walk about the harbour at night, the obvious questions were asked:

> *'When questioned whether or not she thought it safe or wise to venture alone into the harbour in darkness, she replied that she never feared for herself at any time, and had made similar journeys many times before. When asked if she was always alone at those times, she replied that she was.'*

And later,

> *'...she confessed to seeing no one on the quayside, and supposed that she was alone. She did however submit that she heard a sharp report, that could have been a pistol shot, as she was leaving her Office for home, but saw nothing, and felt indisposed to investigate.'*

Did anyone ask why Thomas Grant didn't leave Bristol immediately after supposedly killing Richard? Or why he was there, two nights later, a short distance from Phillipa's office? *She* was there. She says she heard a shot, and she went back home to Charlotte Street. My dark thoughts again: *she arranged for Thomas Grant to kill her husband.* She met him two nights later to pay him what he was owed – the other half, maybe –  according to the Police report it was a very foggy night, so this lucky circumstance would have given her some cover. She took both pistols with her, loaded and ready; two pistols, because the Deringer was apt to fail if not meticulously charged. He took her money, and she shot him, once in the head, took her money back and rolled him into the Float. She threw both pistols after him. Her threat is gone, nobody now to blackmail her, no shared secrets.

That's my conclusion, not theirs. After a further week of investigations they said she was innocent of any blame. The missing pistols were put down to loss or theft, Richard Sparks was likely killed in revenge by Thomas Grant, who himself was assumed murdered by a person or persons unknown, the possibility of suicide never being raised. As I've said, unexplained deaths, even obvious murders, were too common around the harbour in those days, and Phillipa's direct involvement too shocking to contemplate for most –  she was certainly outlandish, but still very respectable.

Thomas was buried in a pauper's grave at St Mary Redcliffe, and Richard at St Andrews, the exclusive church of Clifton's elite; he was apparently a Christian, who'd been happy to marry a wealthy atheist. Phillipa, luckily barred from the funeral by the custom of the age, duly wore her *solemn, unrelieved black* for the required period while taking back the Business she'd given away, as well as lawfully inheriting her husband's money. She followed the rules, mourning – at least outwardly – the loss of Richard Sparks... and my doubts nag without mercy.

Phillipa was a tough character, apparently fearless, and could easily have walked along the Mardyke that night. We know that the pistols were missing, that she went out, and that a man died, but that's all we know for certain of those hours. We also know about her possible need for an heir, and of Richard's wealth, considerable though small compared to hers. So should I throw it away, this preference of mine for her being guilty? It's unlikely ever to be resolved, and I should give her the benefit of the doubt – even she deserves fairness. The truth is, I may have it all quite wrong. She would have taken a big risk of being seen (even with the fog), of being found out, and of being hanged for it... did it all really work so well for her? Or did she employ some other rogue to remove Thomas Grant? Or – surely not – is she entirely innocent, having married Richard Sparks for love, for the child, for companionship, for his abilities and wealth, and the official conclusions were correct? But why would she soon change her name back to Rossetti, which is what happened? Well, the Company was still Rossetti Shipping & Trading rather than Sparks Shipping & Trading (which it may have become) so it kept things tidy, and she saved the expense of reprinting her letterheads...

Too many possibilities, and I'm almost embarrassed at having brought it all up, but it's been interesting; I've striven to implicate my great-grandmother in a foul murder – *two* murders –  which if proven would do great damage to the name of Rossetti, and have unknown consequences for me and my family, even today. My father's sweeter version would have sounded better –  but

I like to think it's possible that somewhere deep in the mud of the Floating Harbour is a pair of 1855 silver-inlaid Philadelphia Deringer pistols... but are they at Welsh Back, or Mardyke? Or were they stolen from Richard Sparks that night after all, and are in someone's attic, or even sitting in a display cabinet somewhere, sleeping quietly with their secrets?

## 13

## MY GRANDMOTHER GEORGINA

The offices of Rossetti Shipping & Trading, later renamed *The Bennett Line* by my father, were a stone's throw from the quayside, nowadays a pleasant tree-lined stretch alongside the Hotwell Road, looking across to the Marina and Brunel's *Great Britain*. A wooden building bought by Pietro in 1788 was rebuilt in Georgian brick in 1792, and that building was much improved by Phillip in 1816 as part of his and John's post-war expansion. The Mardyke quayside, in Pietro and Phillip's early days, was the muddy bank of the tidal river. Proper stone quays appeared in the late 1850s, and the office buildings were later to be cut off from the Float by the Docks Railway and the busy Hotwells Road. It's all gone now, the offices razed and covered with new buildings. There was a time when I could stand on cleared ground, within the lost walls of the room where Phillip, then John and then Phillipa and her short-lived husband would have sat, and later my father. A brief time between demolition and renewal, before all disappeared.

The timber wharves were across the Float, a string of dedicated areas with their old names – Baltic, Onega, Cumberland, Canada, Gefle and Chatham – all stacked high with softwood planks and huge baulks of hardwood, waiting to be hauled away to the shipyards, builder's yards and joinery shops of the West of England. The fresh smell of pine covered the whole area, masking the foul-smelling water, and this was where Phillip Rossetti's ships were unloaded; this was also the view I had when growing up, across the Float to the shipyards and timber wharves, and where as a small child I often crossed in the little boat – always sitting –

when taken on board *North Star* by my father as a treat. Those trips were not usually to the timber wharves though, but further up to Prince's or Wapping, where the sugar and tobacco would be unloaded. I remember hot days there, standing in the shade, keeping out of the way of the men as the cranes swung the sacks and bales around and the heavy smell of raw sugar or tobacco filled the air, with unending noise and movement all around me.

That was my father's world, when steam had overtaken canvas, and the Port was probably at its most efficient. Phillipa's time was different, but no less busy, with scores of men in the holds and on the quayside, manhandling all but the heaviest cargoes. The laboriousness would have been startling to our eyes, the sheer hard work demanded from everyone, young and not-so-young, all in it together.

I think back to my childhood times on the wharves – free, lazy days, marvelling at how and why and what it was all for, and how a ship like *North Star* could go right across the world, being so big... and how could she ever find her way back home?

: : :

Within a week of her husband's death, Phillipa had changed her name, and her daughter's, back to Rossetti (as she was entitled to do) and Sparks disappeared from all but his headstone – the final eradication of her temporary husband, planned or otherwise, but efficient nonetheless; all was tidy again, but I like to think that there were people who were uneasy at how things turned out. Her poor mother simply hid at Brockweir. My father saw nothing to object to and much to praise, as expected: she was just a young woman in mourning making a great effort to keep her Company running.

Georgina Phillipa Elena Sparks – soon to be *Rossetti* – at two months old, knew nothing of the drama around her. She would grow up fatherless, hearing tales of murder and vengeance, of black nights and foul deeds, and of the just suicide of the murderer. The name Sparks would sadly linger forever only on that headstone; he was gone almost without trace, apart from the mixed blood in Georgina's veins, and in her old age she showed me her only tangible link to him – a creased photograph somehow found by her mother shortly before she died and sent to her daughter, then in her fifties, *as a token of my love,* as she put it. Love, perhaps, and better late than never. Richard Sparks was surprisingly delicate-looking, and if I hadn't known of his brashness I would doubt his suitability for Phillipa... but perhaps delicacy suited her more than I imagine.

Her aspirations for Georgina were very clear, even from babyhood, and the young Rossetti spent all her time with a very particular governess, a carefully-chosen woman devoid of religion and softness, an embodiment of Victorian strictness without the religious fervour that usually went with it. This was Miss Gently, an inept name for such a woman as apparently she did nothing gently, except perhaps sleep, but then Georgina never saw her sleeping. Phillipa remembered her own upbringing, and, seeing nothing wrong with how she herself turned out, put the same regime onto her daughter, with the added kindness – as she would put it – of no religion.

Miss Gently was to be her tutor for fifteen years, by which time Phillipa had long given up on her daughter being of the right stuff to follow her in the Business. The child was just not aggressive enough, despite the double onslaught from teacher and mother – she didn't fight like Phillipa had, but instead retreated into herself, as I did with my father... so Georgina and I had a mutual understanding of that particular type of parenting. We shared an almost life-long fear of an abusive, albeit different, parent – both her mother and my father succeeding in frightening and alienating their only child, when just a small amount of love and compassion could have avoided that and given us both quite different futures: what difference would that small amount of love have made to us both?

Georgina missed normal school and was allowed only to mix with children her mother thought suitable, so ended up with no close friends in her earlier years, as the chosen ones were not at all like her. To the slight credit of Phillipa, no doubt after realising her daughter would not shape up as she'd wanted, she allowed the hard-hearted Miss Gently to tone down her dealings with the girl in their later years, and Georgina saw a different side of her tutor: worn down by her ruthless employer, she mellowed a little, and when they parted on Georgina's sixteenth birthday there was an element of relief at having both served under the same mistress and survived. Miss Florence Gently – then in her late forties – became Mrs Florence Burke, and left Bristol for ever, for the sunny shores of Queensland, Australia.

Fifteen years before, when Georgina was a baby and Phillipa wheeled-and-dealed from her office at the Mardyke, Catherine lived in the routine of the Inn, away to the north at Brockweir. Cousin Rhiannon, who by now shared the front rooms with her for company, was a permanent part of the effort there and now almost ran the Inn herself, after the landlord and his wife had moved on some years before. The staff had evolved to the two cousins, a couple of cooks and half-a-dozen serving and cleaning girls, plus the two parrots, Henry and Aku, by now better friends though still kept on different floors.

Rhiannon adored Aku, and intrigued him by talking softly in Welsh as he turned his head to the side, his beady-black eye on her all the while. She was even allowed to hold the sacred broom out from the window some evenings, happily sharing with Catherine the important task of welcoming Aku home again.

Rhiannon, while having a deep friendship with Catherine, apparently found solace in creatures easier than she did with people. She loved those close to her, her tiny circle of friends and family, but communed especially with nature, with creatures of all sizes, in an easy and open way. I have a thin red-covered book on my desk, and inside the cover, below an engraving of a fine-looking woman in flowing robes astride a magnificent white horse, is written, in English and with childish precision -

*RHIANNON.*
*However slowly she rides, other horses cannot catch her.*

This little book is dated 1820, when she was eight, and I know as an odd and distant child she'd greeted strangers with "I am Rhiannon, from the Red Book", and her parents would have to explain that she meant the medieval Welsh *Llyfr Coch Hergest,* the Red Book of Hergest, written four and a half centuries before and containing the older *Mabinogion,* where her name first appears – Rhiannon, the Celtic horse-goddess. Her own red book is filled with pictures of fabulous white horses – only ever white – and added to through her childhood with engravings, sketches and fittingly childish copies of paintings she'd seen. She apparently showed the book to Catherine after being surprised by her while looking at it. I fear she was un-fulfilled, perhaps still happiest wandering in a fourteenth-century world of magical romance; there was a whisper of lost love in her teenage years, but it was never talked about, and it's likely she preferred non-human relationships after that – unconditional, uncomplicated, and reliable. Rhiannon would talk happily with her cousin, but in quiet times would often sit with Aku or Henry, enjoying their worldly innocence and predictability, the perfect comfort of their company.

Both birds were faithful companions to the two women, willing confidants at difficult times, always able to be talked to and great pretenders at understanding; parrots are parrots, and never stop learning, so the vocabulary of both birds flourished over the years though the curious crowds downstairs diminished. When the landlord left he was encouraged to take Henry with him, but chose to leave him in familiar surroundings, and within earshot of his friend upstairs – a selfless act, but Henry suffered with his loss and became quiet for a while as Aku had done after losing Phillip. He was to latch on to Rhiannon as he had to the landlord, and, like Aku, learned some bits of Welsh, but both birds seemed best at picking up stray comments not at all meant for their ears, and repeating them at inappropriate times... *parrots are parrots.*

The Inn was always busy, and then as now the heavy, dark rooms would need lighting most of the day. After Janet's death Phillip had covered up the trendy lighter colours with oak panelling, which he darkened, knowing that Janet preferred the Tudor look to the late Georgian – doors, panelling, some of the floors and all of the ceilings. In those days, the windows were often too small to help with light, so the old Inn would have been lit with candles, and later oil lamps, which is why the ceilings now are almost black, and there's still the overall feeling of heaviness everywhere. Those ancestors of mine moved through rooms, up and down stairs, in and out of doors, stared out of windows and leant against walls and pillars to catch their breath – then as now. The front rooms upstairs had the biggest windows, wide, small-paned, giving good light in the mornings, and I know Catherine would spend many hours sitting there, gazing across the river.

Rhiannon was always around, and much later, as an old woman in her seventies, would spend much time with Phillipa's daughter Georgina, talking wistfully about old times, about parents, grandparents, and the need for love.

Catherine was to die in 1863, and was buried with her beloved Phillip at St Michael's in Abergavenny. She'd seen her three-year-old granddaughter just twice, never going back to Bristol after Phillipa's wedding, not to see her grandchild born, nor to share her early days. She saw her when Phillipa came to Brockweir for some legal matter after Richard Sparks' death and again – apparently as a treat – on the baby's first birthday, but never to be repeated. Catherine was sixty-one when she died, not a great age even then, and I fear a very unhappy woman, no doubt feeling she was reaping what she'd helplessly sown with her daughter. *Too late, too late,* she'd once said to Rhiannon, wishing for time to rewind and give her a second chance.

Her will left the Inn in trust to the almost-unknown Georgina, a three-year-old who would inherit at twenty-one; if she died before that age the Inn would go to Rhiannon, who anyway was to be given a generous allowance on Catherine's death. Phillipa was to be denied at all costs, and her mother was sure of her cousin; such wills were open to abuse, and the child could have become even worse than her mother, so the risk was taken on Catherine's scant memories and her hopes for the beautiful, sadly-missed baby. Apart from her happiness with Phillip, her life was, I believe, one mostly of sadness; her daughter turned out so wrongly and went on to cause such unhappiness to so many, that it was difficult to redeem her –  and it was all Catherine's fault (or so she believed, in her heart). Rhiannon's faithfulness and love for her cousin would make sure that Georgina owned the Inn when her time came, however she turned out, and that became a huge comfort for her – she never gave up hope that the little girl would somehow defy her mother's ambitions for her and turn out well. I wish –  and I have many such wishes – she could have foreseen Georgina's defiance, and so feel some genuine hope for the future of the Rossettis.

In 1876, on her sixteenth birthday, Georgina's studies came to an end. Her preoccupied mother was at the office every day, usually returning to eat dinner with her in the early evening, where the topics of conversation were few and struggled to stray from business matters, which Phillipa's head was full of. She didn't know how to connect with her daughter, so most meals were eaten in silence with the odd trite comment. Georgina's opinions and wishes were not required, and she voiced them at her peril. During the day she was expected to make herself useful somehow, and soon turned into one of those good Clifton ladies who helped the poor, to the disdain of her mother, who believed the poor should help themselves. As I've said, she'd given up with her daughter, who didn't matter to her apart from being respectable.

So at sixteen years old, Georgina thought about her future. In her old age she told me she'd felt free for the first time, and could leave the house whenever she liked, free from Miss Gently's timetables. She found friends at last, and followed them into the charitable works of girls and ladies in no need of being paid. The wealthy of Bristol were gathered on the hill around her, with Clifton offering the best new houses and the most reputable surroundings, but it was in the next couple of years that her disillusions with the people she mixed with became too much to bear: she had one special friend – Eliza Armstrong – but few others, and she mostly saw empty-headed women, socialites intent on furthering themselves by spending more money and gossiping about those beneath them, their husbands rich bores obsessed with image. Status was all, and though Georgina admitted to being somewhat spoiled, she never joined that set, all of whom were also avid churchgoers, an option closed to her by her mother. She would also have been aware of the tone of Clifton, which was startling – *'Why must the common people be allowed to walk about here?'* asked one letter-writer, and another, *'We have nothing common or unclean among us at present.'* They had no fear of voicing their opinions in those days.

Georgina hated her mother's indifference to the *unworthy poor* – which covered just about all of those in poverty in the City – and, feeling like an outsider, she decided to clear her head of Bristol and move to Brockweir. "I ran away from all that," she told me, "and it doesn't make me proud."

She'd visited the Inn a few years before, and been surprised to learn from Rhiannon that it was coming to her – her mother never having mentioned it. The thought of owning the Inn wasn't exciting to her at first – she was already wealthy, after all – but during those years of freedom in Bristol it gradually became so and she began to look forward to life in the Wye Valley, feeling certain that her time in Bristol, and especially with her mother, would come to an end. She made her move soon after her eighteenth birthday, but took her fear of that mother with her – she would not entirely lose it for another thirty-six years.

: : :

Phillipa Rossetti's company thrived. Sugar and tobacco were the staple cargoes, and in the first decades after 1860 nothing much changed. Her rules of business were simple: pay your captains and your mates well, and your ordinary seamen as little as possible –  that way things keep running, as unhappy men were easily replaced, and the important ones were kept happy. Obvious, and not far from the ideal truth for many businesses, even these days – the difference being that men were cheap, expendable, and plentiful. She had replaced John Parrish's captains, and most of his crews, in the months after taking over, preferring to have her own men rather than those who remembered John and could be resentful. She had also sold all three of Phillip's ships in 1862 – *Montclair, Pensive* and *Anna Elena* went very cheaply because of their age, and were replaced by three larger vessels, younger, but not as strong nor as well-maintained as those first three. She would find that her new ships would not last long, but her eyes saw more profit in bigger cargoes, and she worked them harder than ever.

Unfairness was in most things she touched – her greed saw to that. A typical example was on trips to the West Indies, where ordinary seamen were encouraged to take half their wages on arrival there, which was attractive to men having been on board, on poor rations, for around six weeks... the advantage in this for Phillipa was that their wages would be paid in local currency, one pound for one pound, but that local pound was worth less than sterling – which was tolerated as life was cheaper there. It was a method she encouraged long after it had died out elsewhere, and it always seemed to work for men desperate to spend money.

Apart from handsomely-paid favourites and poorly-paid sailors, she encouraged fines during voyages for damage to cargo, but under such vague terms that it was impossible to argue against, and the injustice would have to be lived with if a man was to keep his job or survive the trip without harm. All of this made her more wealthy as the years went by, and as long as men were easily available, they could be wooed on board with false promises from the silver tongues of her captains and mates. They were all in it together, and of course, she would have happily carried slaves as well had she been around a hundred years before. Her unjust methods were also observed by other traders at Bristol who were not impressed – not that their concerns would bother her, but she would soon be forced to take notice and change her ways.

This was during the 1880s, and I'm sure it was the guardians of Bristol's wealth, the Merchant Venturers, who stopped her. Had she been a man, Phillipa would certainly have tried to join them, but as a woman it was impossible. She was looked upon with curiosity when she began, followed by a certain admiration, then tolerance, then with outright hostility from some. She was wealthy and successful, the right requirements for the Port, but her reputation was not good and her methods were seen to be unfair in the enlightenment of the late 1800s: *she will have to change her ways, if she wants to stay here.* The message reached her, and I get a small amount of pleasure imagining something actually being forced upon her, of her having to rethink her strategy.

This came at the time when her ships were becoming tired, having been pushed too hard and maintained too little. For a businesswoman, she was lacking in caring for her assets, both ships and men, and the choice she had in 1882 was to replace her ships like for like, or to leap into the heady new age of steam.

The Merchant Venturer involvement was revealed to Georgina on one of her rare visits to Bristol, by a too-familiar office clerk who would have lost his job if Phillipa had found out... but the attractive twenty-two-year-old must have turned his head, and made him careless: "She's thinking about steamers," he'd said, and, "The Merchants are watching her."

That second revelation was depressing.

She'd actually been invited by her mother to stay for a few days at Charlotte Street in a golden September – this was three years after she'd left Bristol, and it would be nice to think that Phillipa missed her daughter, but it's more likely she had other reasons. Georgina went, warily, but looking forward to Bristol rather than her mother, who anyway left the house every day just as before. Phillipa told her about her plans to change sail for steam, and seemed eager to share her ambitions – very unlike her – so the invitation was probably meant to impress with her plans and to ward off any rumours of pressure from high places that may reach Brockweir.

The dinner-table talk was little improved, but she'd coped better with the familiar coldness, spending her days visiting friends and familiar places in the town. She'd heard rumours around Bristol during that visit, stories and whisperings, all pointing to her mother being under pressure from certain people there, people with great influence, and in Bristol that usually meant the Merchant Venturers. Phillipa had fainter connections with those people, and may have been unaware of their depth of feelings, but anyway would have been furious with Georgina for even dipping her toes, albeit innocently, into her affairs. Georgina left Charlotte Street the next day without giving anything away, but the fact was that her mother was in peril of losing her trade at Bristol unless she impressed the people that mattered.

Within six months, two almost-new steamships were bought as the three old ships were sold off. The fact that her reputation also improved is proof that she was forced to be a better employer – the wealthy merchants wanted the best reputation for Bristol's traders, and rogue operators – especially female ones – would not be tolerated. It seems Phillipa needed to conform and impress, so she did, and came through safely.

The sailing ships of the Rossettis were gone, and the era of steam had arrived. Phillipa's smart new steel ships – the forerunners of my *North Star* – with the novel screw propellers rather than side paddles, would shorten the westward Atlantic voyage to just ten days, with fewer men and greater comfort for all. *William & Rose* and *Roderick*, both from Clyde shipyards, would serve her well and take her into the new century, into my father's time.

## 14

## THE BEGUILING OF MY FATHER

*Brockweir,*
*25th October, 1882*

*Dearest Mother,*
*I trust that you are well, and that Your Business is*
*satisfactory.*
*I wish to inform You of my intention to marry*
*Arthur Bennett on Wednesday the 15th of February*
*next, at the Register Office in Thornbury, at 11 o'clock.*
*Both Arthur and myself earnestly wish for You to be*
*with us on that day, and to join us in a modest*
*Celebration of our Vows.*
*I am aware of Your commitments in Bristol, but We*
*are both firm in our desire to see You on that day, and*
*hope that You may find a way to attend.*

*With fond assurances,*
*Your daughter Georgina.*

Eight days later, the same letter came back, with the words
*"That will not be possible"* written across the bottom, below
Georgina's signature. The letter is in front of me now, and
also the envelope, which is addressed by someone else, no
doubt to save Phillipa the trouble.

When Georgina first showed me this letter, in 1933, she
let me read it, then asked for my thoughts. I was nineteen
and on my first return visit from College in London, calling
at Brockweir to see my ageing grandmother again after a
long absence. She was still living at the Inn with her

husband Arthur. I read the letter again. I remember saying something like *I'm surprised you even invited her, when you didn't get on with her at all.*

She said she'd tried because of Arthur, who couldn't believe her terrible tales – he'd never met her, but Phillipa was her mother, after all. Georgina was sure it would be a waste of time, but asked her all the same, because of Arthur wanting her to be better than he'd been told she was. Her choice of Thornbury, just north of Bristol, was chosen to make it easier for her mother to attend, without having to cross the Severn.

I said I was glad she tried, and sorry her mother didn't have the time or the wish to reply properly, not even wanting to keep her daughter's letter. I understood the sadness of it all, especially the Register Office part. She'd joined the Church of England the year before (being a safe distance from her mother) and she and Arthur went to St Michael's at Tintern every Sunday, so forgoing a wedding there must have been very difficult. She told me how they'd talked endlessly about it, and how profound a decision it was for her to allow her mother the chance of taking away from them the most special and meaningful day of their lives in that little church by the river. It would have been so difficult, she said, and for once her mother's unkindness was a relief.

*That will not be possible* was sad good news for Georgina, and proof for Arthur of Phillipa's lack of affection for his beloved. They'd both tried hard with her, and given her a chance of redemption. If Arthur had been a wealthy businessman, someone she could respect, she would have come to their wedding, wherever it was, but he wasn't. He was the son of a Monmouth grocer; he was kind, good-looking, sensible and practical – all of those things, but *too* kind, and with a weak head for business, so no more to be said, close the book on him. Close the book on them both.

They were married on that fifteenth of February, but in Tintern, not Thornbury. And she'd worn the silver necklace that Catherine had refused and Phillipa didn't care about; after wearing it all that day it was put back in its box, upstairs in Phillip's old study, in familiar surroundings. It had been a clear and sunny day, the first of many for them, and after the short drive from the church to the Inn they left in the afternoon, on the hour's journey to their friends at the Manor of St Pierre, near Chepstow, where they spent a happy three days away from the distractions of Brockweir.

The previous year *The Wondrous Gift* had become Georgina's on her twenty-first birthday, with a minimum of fuss: a short visit by Catherine's old and very upright solicitor, a few signatures, a celebratory drink with Rhiannon – job done. She was a wealthy property owner, a young lady of even more means, and after her wedding she would share it all with her husband Arthur, genuinely, and with affection. I can't imagine her mother understanding that a bond of love could work in such an arrangement, or that a husband could be trusted that much – *but she did marry Richard Sparks.*

: : :

Sarah Rossetti Bennett was born on a chilling December day in the year they married, a day of settling snow, of roaring fires and celebration, and was the first girl to take the Rossetti name, a wish of her great-grandmother Catherine. Rhiannon knew that her cousin longed to continue Phillip's name, and it would be kind to her memory if the new child were to begin that tradition. Georgina was there before her, and did not need persuading. But Sarah was not strong; her early years were a continual round of illness that no amount of care would avoid, and by the time her brother Richard arrived a year later she'd twice missed a very early death, first from pneumonia and then from malnutrition, having stopped feeding for almost a week. Richard Bennett was stronger, a robust healthy child, and when their third arrived the first two had become an odd couple, one always ill, the other quite the opposite. The third child was my father Peter – equally robust – and the three Bennetts, each a year apart from each other, grew up in the busy confines of the Inn while their grandmother Phillipa kept to her isolation in Bristol.

Georgina talked of sunny days at Brockweir; always *sunny* days, as if they were all put aside for her alone to remember. She would often begin with, "I remember one lovely sunny day..." and go on to tell me of times which didn't really need sunshine to be memorable. It was just her way – it simply made the memory better, and probably sprang from that first unforgettable day of sunshine when she'd married Arthur. Even much later, after the sadnesses that awaited her had come and gone, she clung to the backdrop of the sunny day.

The first of these sadnesses was when Aku died. Sarah was four years old, and the boys very lively toddlers, when Aku left them. He'd lived for more than sixty years, a wise old bird who'd seen so much, who'd conversed with Phillip Rossetti, his wife Catherine, daughter Phillipa and grand-daughter Georgina, through to his great-grandson – my father – and been witness to the lives of many others. He bridged the years from his master's sad times at Brockweir – he was the wondrous gift who never knew his intended mistress – right through the trials of young Phillipa to the boisterous atmosphere of the Bennett children growing up. His younger companion Henry had died ten years before, still a good age for a parrot. They were always separated, on different floors, but within sound of each other, and they both suffered with the departure of those close to them; it was a blessing that Aku died before Rhiannon, his oldest friend. This was not the end of parrots at Brockweir, however... some seventy years later my daughter Elena would find a new Aku, and put him in the same cage in the same room – Phillip Rossetti's bedroom and study at the front of the Hotel.

Richard and Peter were first taught at home, and when they were eight they were sent to school in Monmouth, but Sarah stayed at the Inn where her parents could watch over her. In their free time, and later during the summer months when school had stopped, the boys charged around, filling up their days with adventures, testing their anxious parents. In and out of the river, in and out of boats, roaring through the forest above the Inn and staying out far too long for their mother's comfort – all in stark contrast to my own compliant and isolated childhood thirty years later in Bristol, my less hectic days of growing up.

In 1891, before Richard started school at Monmouth, Georgina had taken her three children to Bristol to visit their grandmother, with predictable results. Phillipa, having no skill with children, tolerated them. She'd commented on Sarah's frailty, suggesting a stronger routine might improve her health, but Georgina knew all about stronger routines, and ignored her. Poor Sarah was to die two years later, just before her eleventh birthday, after a November sore throat turned into rheumatic fever. The child slipped quietly to a death expected since babyhood then half-expected as she seemed to improve in the warmth of each summer, and the blow was heavy when it came. Her brothers were shocked into quietness. They were used to her up-and-down life, but could not be prepared (as their parents were) for the brutal reality of losing her. She was buried at the quiet Tintern church, close to Janet, her great-grandfather's first wife, and her grave became a place of acceptance for her parents, and sad bewilderment for her brothers in the years ahead. Much later my father Peter would deride his sister's failings, even comparing her usefulness to mine, but I accept that he was far gone from humanity by then.

On that visit to their grandmother Phillipa, the boys were too quiet and conspiratorial. They were always in awe of her, which she seemed to enjoy, but everyone was relieved when the visit was over. They'd looked around Clifton and walked down to the harbour, where at last the boys found things to interest them – one of Phillipa's captains allowed them all on board *William & Rose*, and they would never forget the overpowering smell of tobacco everywhere. Georgina told me that they soon forgot the boring parts (mostly their time at the house in Charlotte Street) and often asked for another visit –  but it would be four years before they returned to Bristol.

Georgina's best friend from her Clifton days, Eliza Armstrong, was the also-married daughter of an engineer whose own father made a fortune building ships through Bristol's busiest years, and his interest and profits nowadays were in the new steam engines which would soon replace sails. Eliza and Georgina were like-minded about most things; they were firm writing companions, and in July 1896 a letter came to Brockweir inviting the two boys to Clifton, as friends for Eliza's own son James –  he was the same age as Richard –  and to show them the Bristol they hadn't properly seen.

Georgina worried over it, fearing the closeness of her mother, but decided to let them go, Arthur going along for safekeeping on the journey. Since their visit to Phillipa, four years before, nothing at all had come from Bristol –  no news, nothing – so Georgina reasoned that her mother was absorbed in the Business, as ever, and would leave her grandsons alone – if she knew they were there at all, that is.

They went, early on a bright August morning, and after politely spending a little time with their hosts Arthur left again for home. The youngsters were apparently happy to stay, for the first time in their lives, with strangers –  and that was the very beginning of my father's development, his slow poisoning in the atmosphere of Clifton and just within reach of the grasping fingers of his grandmother Phillipa. His year-older brother Richard would fare better, by not being the favourite. They enjoyed Bristol. Eliza allowed the boys to go out in the care of her son James, after very strict warnings about behaviour and timings, and he took them everywhere, from the grand streets of Clifton to the less-salubrious areas around the Floating Harbour, and through Queen Square, the oasis of opulence almost enclosed by the scruffy quays and backs. The same streets that had bored them the first time became exciting with James as their guide. They surveyed the harbour from Redcliffe Parade, dodged along the noisy wharves, crossed back over the lock gates above the grey mud at Cumberland – oblivious to the terrible drop to the water at low tide – then climbed the hill back to the safety of Clifton.

The Armstrongs lived at Royal York Crescent, probably the most excellent address in Bristol –  an impressive sweep of Georgian town houses overlooking the City and the Somerset hills beyond, and a short walk from Sion Hill where they would have looked across to the bridge that would become so special to me – all of this at the centre of respectability and wealth. This was very different to their lives at Brockweir, and they came back with tales of excess that bemused Georgina and Arthur, sobering stories of grandness mixed in with their boyish excitement.

But Phillipa had somehow known they were there, and her interest was kindled – or rekindled – which lead to her contacting them. The first letters from her arrived in September, one for each grandson. Georgina was alarmed and read them secretly when she could; they were strange, she thought, because of their ordinariness, their lack of coldness, of preaching or suggestion, beyond urging both boys to write back. She would never have thought her mother could be so unthreatening to anyone. It was out of character, and it worried her. Nevertheless, after asking what their grandmother had written, she herself urged them to respond, out of politeness. Small talk was thus answered by small talk, but she couldn't imagine her mother giving such trivia any time at all. It was all wrong, and suspicious... Phillipa was after them, grooming them, surely – but was her daughter mistaken? And if not, what to do? But it was too obvious, and inevitable. Georgina expected to inherit the business – whether she wanted to run it or not (she told me she didn't) – but if she didn't get it then either Richard – or Peter – would. To succeed, they'd need to work with Phillipa for the years before she retired – that made sense. But Georgina simply couldn't face losing them to the person she feared and distrusted most, and certainly not so soon. When her sons reached their twenties, maybe, *but don't start now, not at thirteen... or twelve.*

As the months passed and the letters kept coming, she realised that her son Peter – it had to be Peter – was indeed being inducted little by little into the world of his grandmother, the world of Rossetti Shipping & Trading. She was perplexed, wanting to keep her boys close, but couldn't see how to do it. Forbidding contact with their inheritance would never work.

Richard was the less serious of the two, more happy-go-lucky, more focused on having a good time than Peter, who would often stop and think, and analyse. And Peter was much better with money. Although they were each getting their own letters, he would be the one to follow Phillipa, and Georgina couldn't see how to cut her ties with her and the Company. It wasn't possible.

The letters continued; this was one of the first ones, sent in November 1896 to her twelve-year-old grandson:

*"My Dear Peter,*

*I have received your October letter, and am very pleased that you will continue with our monthly exchanges. I have written separately to your brother, though I fear he is becoming bored with me and my questions and requests! If he talks to you about me, please reassure him that I write only out of a genuine interest in him and his affairs, and I do not intend, nor wish, to bore him. Urge him to continue, as I find his letters, as I find yours, so very interesting. As you are aware, I am alone in Bristol, and therefore find great comfort in reading of your lives at Brockweir.*

*You have asked many questions about my Company, and I am gratified that you should be so interested in the everyday workings of what will one day be your mother's Business, and then your brother's, or yours.*

*This is a great encouragement for me, to think that you could be the owner of this Company in the years to*

*come, and that you could move it forward to the benefit
of our family..."*

After a few months, the letters became more polarised. Richard's stayed at their pedestrian level while Peter's reached out to areas beyond the interests of boys. The changes were subtle, but because Georgina feared them she saw them straightaway. She picked the words apart while the boys were at school and as there was nothing secret in them they were never hidden – Richard's were left in a pile on his desk, awaiting his reluctant replies, and Peter's were kept in a drawer in some tidiness.  What Georgina never knew was what the boys wrote in reply.

: : :

The new year, 1897, was made worse by a death in the family. The passing of Rhiannon, the cousin who came to help, and stayed, was a great loss to them all. She never married, and apart from that hint of lost love in her teens which she herself never spoke of, there was no love in her life beyond the people – and parrots – she lived with and her family further north. Georgina, Arthur and the boys stood sadly around as her coffin was carried from the Inn and placed on a hearse, behind two perfectly black and black-plumed horses, and taken to the Catholic Church at Monmouth. From there she went to the graveyard at St Michael's in Abergavenny where her parents were, and Catherine and Phillip. She'd met Phillip when he was courting Catherine, and saw them married at that same Monmouth church. She was among friends, and loved ones.

: : :

Richard and Peter had for some years been sent every day to Monmouth School, a daily half-mile with the pony and trap to Tintern Station, then the short trip following the river up to Troy, where they changed trains for Mayhill, and walked over the bridge to the school. The railway had arrived twenty years before, opening up the valley with regular runs to Chepstow and Monmouth, and Georgina remembered pleasant family outings on the train in the lovely summers. Her rose-tinted memories were full of those lovely summers, of hot afternoons in the sun-trap of the garden, and the general happiness of her situation, even after the loss of Sarah.

Since the birth of the boys, and through their growing-up in the last two decades of the old century, many of those remembered outings were to Monmouth, visiting Arthur's parents at their home above their shop in Church Street at the top end of town. This was a treat for all – always a Sunday afternoon, and they would take the train to Troy and Mayhill, as their schoolboy sons did, and walk up through the streets to the busy thoroughfare where E Bennett, Grocer, had his shop. The street was busy on Sundays, when fine weather saw the elegantly-dressed Monmouth ladies parading beneath summer parasols beside their gentlemen, and sailor-suited boys and girls.

There was music in the square, and walks along the river and through the park and the Sunday streets, a different and more relaxed place than the weekday market town. There were cakes and tea to be had, and Georgina would usually insist on paying for treats; it was a fact that she was wealthy, and she simply encouraged her hosts to accept it without feeling humiliated – they were not poor, but certainly felt so in her presence. "I wanted to help them," she told me, "I wanted to pay my way, and sometimes theirs, without them being hurt." And by extension, of course, their only son was also wealthy – they no doubt found it easier to accept help from Arthur.

Lilian and Edward Bennett's rooms were reached via a narrow staircase at the side of the shop, and Arthur had been embarrassed the first time at this less-than-respectable entrance to his family home; this was soon after their marriage, but his new wife was unfazed, and fell in well with her new relations, the couple that would become a worthy replacement for her own missing father and absent mother. She came to love the smallness of their home – a tidy, welcoming place where life was warm and easy-going, and without expectations. Lilian and Edward took some time to relax in her company: it was common, even expected, that many rich ladies would put on airs (Georgina wouldn't have known how to) but after visiting Brockweir for the wedding and after, the elder Bennetts had seen no falseness in her. Nevertheless I would think that Arthur's parents were in some anxiety over her first visit to them, but I'll always remember Arthur's comment to me, "She was so refreshing, not a threat at all", and this was a testament to Georgina's generous and fair nature, as everyone, rich or poor, was given the same importance.

Her wealth never got in the way of her judgment of people; in time it seems everyone accepted her, while still being in awe of her, which she couldn't do much about. She would dress down for those visits to Monmouth, not needing to impress with finery, to compete with the local gentry in their Sunday best... small wonder her mother was uninterested in her.

Through all this time Phillipa was playing a very long game with Peter, so as not to alarm his parents – but she failed, as Georgina slowly accepted that she could do nothing to stop him being drawn in before his time, as she put it. The letters still came, but no more to Richard, whose mind was set on the Royal Navy, and therefore not useful to his grandmother. Those letters were by then quite open in their intentions, and Peter proudly showed them to his parents as proof of his being the chosen one, the successor; they never mentioned his mother, their whole tone now fitting in with Georgina's fears for him, and perfectly fitting her mother. They felt there was nothing they could do. Their son was already showing the arrogance that would define the rest of his life, full only of self-promotion, uncaring about his parents' concerns or wellbeing. Arthur, by now properly in dread of Phillipa, had to let his son run his course. "My husband has always been a good man," said Georgina, "but his influence with Peter was slight." But Georgina went along with Arthur, so both avoided confrontation and waited for the inevitable: for Peter to inherit instead of her, and in truth she was not angry, not mad with her mother – she surprised herself with her acceptance of things. She felt she could let the Business go, but her son – could she let him go? She told me, "The Business was not to be mine. I wasn't bitter – I thought it was for the greater good. It was all for the best because it would give us a happier life, and we were as wealthy as we would ever need to be. Was I stupid not to fight? I don't think so. The Business was wrong for me, so I let it go, put it out of my mind. But letting go of Peter was hard. He was my son."

When he was fifteen, that son had been invited to Bristol by Phillipa, rather than by Eliza, who'd had both boys the previous summers. Georgina was not able to prevent this beguiling of Peter: "She had him at fifteen," she told me, "and we lost him at fifteen."

## 15

## MY MOTHER ALICIA

'*In 1899, at fifteen years old, I left My family at Brockweir and travelled to Bristol, with the intention of learning from My Grandmother the rudiments of the Business She had so successfully built. I carried with Me great excitement and Ambition for My future in this Business. Her kindness to Me those two weeks, I hope I have repaid in full. My family were much in Admiration of My efforts and encouraged Me. My Mother especially told Me of Her wish for Me to have the Business after My Grandmother. I shall always be grateful for the confidence She instilled into My youthful character and Her understanding concerning the best way forward, as My Brother Richard had no ambitions in that direction. All of these wishes were a revelation to Me.*'

A revelation? Not at all. A fabrication.

His mother was dead when he wrote that, so he could say what he liked – he only ever quoted dead people. He never mentioned his wife Alicia, nor Arthur, nor Clara and me, and any objections from those who'd known the no-longer-living when they were alive would be ignored, or shouted down.

He came back from Charlotte Street full of self-importance, an obnoxious teenager, back to the boredom of home and school and parents. He made it clear that life held more for him than Brockweir could offer, and he would tolerate everything and everyone around him until he could leave for Bristol, and stay there. His mother Georgina told me those years were the saddest for her – more so than the long struggle with Sarah, which was somehow a natural process – because of the way she herself was overlooked for Peter, and because of the way he contrived to capitalise on anything for his own good. From that time on, the inheritance was never discussed, and she learned the facts from her son's boasting. There was silence from Bristol.

His grandmother evidently approved of Monmouth School, otherwise Peter would probably have been taken out and put into one of the many in Clifton. In any case, she insisted he leave at seventeen, and come to Bristol, and that was when Georgina was formally told – through a letter to Peter – of her mother's plans. He would have the Business after Phillipa, and his mother would have a *sufficient* amount of money, which was expected to replace any hopes she may have had. The money would come soon, excluding her from the Business and leaving the way open for Peter to inherit in due course without inter-ference. The money was substantial, and came via the Company solicitor along with the documents she had to sign. She was bought out, paid off, written off. She did not fight. She was, in reality, content to be free of the old Rossetti Business at last – and of her mother, who would finally cut all ties; it was worth it, and they would keep the other Rossetti Business at Brockweir. So they went with the flow, and when Peter was taken out of school, it was too hard for her and Arthur, simply too hard, to insist otherwise. Their son was lost to Bristol.

They still had Richard, and when Peter left, life was without doubt better. They settled back into a different, kinder routine, going into their forties with lighter hearts and much relief. Bristol and all it meant was gone, out of mind at least – and Georgina never went back while her mother was alive; she missed her son though, as she knew she would.

Peter had spent the two summers before his seventeenth

birthday with his grandmother, his brother staying at Brockweir, having decided against the regular stay with James and Eliza at Clifton. Richard knew he was losing his brother, and found new friends. He was not to forget James, and after Peter left he invited him to Brockweir, as much a sea-change in environment for James as Bristol had been for him. Their interests and ambitions were linked, and they would both join the Navy, going to war in the same ship in 1915.

: : :

So in 1901, as *The New Century of Progress* began, Bristol became my seventeen-year-old father's home. He lived in Charlotte Street, in the front room I would one day have, and he shared the house with his grandmother, a housekeeper and a cook. His days were spent in the office at Mardyke Wharf, at a desk next to his mentor; she puffed at cheroots most of the time – she'd started smoking soon after the death of her husband – and there were people who thought she must be half man to do that. It was bad enough not to go to church, even if your heart wasn't in it, but for a woman to smoke was just too appalling for most. It was exotic, in the worst sense, and her reputation went beyond salvation. People would stare at the half-man – godless, husbandless, depraved – and apparently she couldn't have cared less.

It seems Peter took to the Business easily. According to the True Account that he would much later involve himself with, he was a modest genius – unlikely, unless he'd very much changed during the first five years he was there, five years away from anyone to tell us anything about him. Nothing exists from those years, just his own writings, mostly about himself, to make any judgement – so we must ignore his self-praise and assume he was the same Peter who left Brockweir, or a worse one. I'd bet on the latter. There was no reason for him to improve his morals, but an excellent one for them to become worse – and that was the influence of his grandmother.

She ran the Business well, if you look at the profits, and her early specialisation on sugar had shifted to tobacco. Two huge bonded warehouses were built by the Corporation in 1902, to take the swelling imports from North America, and this gave her a boost – she could now bring as much tobacco across as she was able to, and the Port would handle it all. That's much simplified, of course; she was one of many doing the same thing, and she had to be very astute over which cargo at which time, sometimes reverting to sugar or molasses, sometimes even the odd cargo of timber, and sometimes cotton. In other words, shipping was not straightforward if you wanted the maximum profit, which everyone did. She was hard and unyielding to competitors, her reputation racing ahead of her in everything, and this gave her an edge over anyone showing even slight weakness or hesitation. It wouldn't surprise me if *Beware of Mrs Rossetti* was the first advice for anyone starting their trade there.

She advised Peter during that time, according to his *True Account*, to marry someone wealthy. As a business move, it was sensible: a bride with her own or her parents' money – preferably her own – and a watertight marriage contract. The law had changed in 1882, so unlike Phillipa's own marriage to the unfortunate Richard Sparks, a woman now kept her assets upon marriage, but if she could be persuaded to invest in the Company it would be all to the good… he makes the comment that it may be of benefit to all if his wife were of independent means. He began to look for this wife, preferably non-religious, and early in 1906 he met Alicia Francome, the daughter of a landowner, from Tuffley, below Robin's Wood Hill on the southern edge of Gloucester. Unfortunately, she was religious, but her wealth helped him to overcome that. Someone had thought it through though, surely: in case she was religious – and I imagine wealthy, accessible atheists to be very thin on the ground in those days – she should not be from Bristol, because the likely church wedding would not be convincing, as grandson and grandmother were known for their lack of faith. Better to return quietly to Bristol as husband and wife.

Alicia was twenty-one, had received her fortune and was ripe for the picking... and a young, wealthy man with great ambition and promise was enough to convince her parents that he was the right one. What her feelings were, we'll never know, but I hope the girl who would be my mother was happy. They married in September 1906, in the Anglican church at Sandhurst, above Gloucester, Phillipa probably entering her first church for many years, and all in the name of greed. The celebrations were at Alicia's family house at Tuffley, a suitably imposing place, and I guess Phillipa and Peter answered the inevitable questions about their lives in Bristol – especially about churches and social life – with lies and fabrications, as they'd no doubt done during the parents' visit to Bristol during the months of the engagement. And Phillipa probably kept off the cheroots for the day. None of it would really matter: disillusionment would soon follow for Alicia, and maybe protestations from her parents, but they would all be efficiently dealt with. Those two were actors after all, and actors are always able to mask the truth about themselves; I know that Peter went with his wife occasionally to one of the small out-of-town churches, for the sake of appearances – but only occasionally. He allowed her to follow her faith, and sometimes joined in when it suited some purpose. Acting, and dishonesty, from a man comfortable in his beliefs, and I wonder how he lived with his twisted and sad certainties about others; those were also the days of the Suffragist struggle, and there were many heated meetings around Clifton – I'm aware of my father's thoughts regarding those women, even while praising his grandmother, also a woman.

Georgina and Arthur first became aware of their younger son's marriage five days after it happened, via a letter from Alicia's parents, consoling them for having to miss the wedding. The shocking truth is that they were not there because they had not been invited, nor even informed of it. My father's soft-headed mother and her grocer's son husband were well below the acceptable level of refinement.

∴ ∴ ∴

Alicia and Peter Bennett moved into Eighteen Charlotte Street on the evening of the fifteenth of September, 1906 – a Saturday, the day of their wedding, and it was raining. There was no new house for them. Phillipa had spent two months and a lot of money in converting her house into what she thought was suitable for two families, with children in mind. She closed off her upstairs rooms, gave herself a private staircase, and contrived to avoid the distractions of the newlyweds by banning them from her living space, and insisting they eat in their own rooms.

The work was shoddy and cheap on Alicia's side; it was temporary-looking, and incongruous. The plain new partitions pushed against the Georgian wall panelling with no attempt at blending or friendliness, cutting across patterned wooden floors, cutting the landing in half.

Phillipa spent money and saved money, showing off her meanness – the quality was important, but only on her own side where the finish was better, with cornices, dados and skirting boards matching what was there. What Peter really thought of this enforced privacy is not recorded, but he praises her sensitivity & forethought. And the poor housekeeper was thus suddenly overstretched, as was the cook, but they had to go along with things to keep their jobs.

Alicia – my mother – soon realised that she was expected to support the Business by giving it her money, but she insisted on giving only half of her inheritance. And it was bearable, because within two months a third ship was bought, and it made a big difference to see something real rather than having her money disappear into the melting pot. She secretly took on the newcomer, the steamship *Angel*, as her own, as some comfort to her both in name and substance, as something she'd helped to buy. She would always be her ship, her contribution, and she prayed she would not be renamed by her new owners – but *Angel* was to keep both her name and Alicia's affection.

Her life at Charlotte Street was generally forlorn. She was convinced it took two years to become pregnant because of the anxiety in being married to Peter Bennett. Two years, before her body either hardened, softened or gave in – she was never sure which – before her child could start, and she shyly confided to me that it wasn't for the want of trying. That's a few sentences to describe a couple of years of neglect while her husband forged ahead with what interested him, namely profit, and it was only when their son, my lost brother Peter Phillip, was born in 1909 that she managed to feel a little appreciated. The child was doted on by his father, and she took some comfort from that; she said he was a changed man. I suspect he'd changed into a man who'd found treasure and looked forward to investing it... but that's cruel. Surely there was also love, genuine love of some kind for his son, over and beyond his pride and ambitions?

Alicia hung on to her fifty percent inheritance. Keeping most of it outside Bristol, on her father's advice, it would always be *her* money, not Bennett money, not Rossetti money. Before twelve months had passed she knew the score, she knew how her life would be with those cheerless grasping people. If she died before her husband, all would go back to her own family in Gloucester, not to them. Such necessities made her sad, not to be trusting, nor to have good wishes for her new family... but she never felt any love coming her way, just transparent dishonesty when they wanted something from her that would benefit them, that couldn't be got by insistence. She would go on to balance this lack of affection with friendships among her neighbours, and also with her mother-in-law Georgina at Brockweir, when she was at last allowed to go there.

## 16

## COMINGS & GOINGS

Bristol in the early nineteen-hundreds was very different from a hundred years before, when the Rossettis were settling in and Phillip was a teenager finding his way. Steamships now outnumbered sailing ships, and after almost a thousand years of constant use the harbour would soon lose trade to the new docks, downriver at Avonmouth. The unimproved seven-mile approach was becoming not worth the effort for most, and the landlocked, isolated Floating Harbour began its long downward slide; but there was still a long time before the container ships at Avonmouth would finally close the Port to any worthwhile cargoes, and my father would slog on in uncertain times through the decades to the second war, never making a loss. He was a capable captain, for sure.

Life went on at Charlotte Street, and at Brockweir – busy times, and the lead-up to the first war was remembered by my grandmother as more rosy than perhaps it was. Her disruptive son had left the Inn, and she and Arthur went through their fifth decades in some happiness, with their other son Richard back and fore during his naval training. In 1910, four years after Peter's marriage, Richard was twenty-six, at the Royal Naval College in Dartmouth, and looking forward to living his dream of a life on the ocean wave.

My mother Alicia became a regular visitor to the Inn, after my father and his dreadful grandmother gave her permission to go. They had to let her visit her parents, but Brockweir was somehow a step too far for them. Probably they feared Georgina telling tales. She could have gone anyway, but preferred to slowly chip away at their opposition rather than show too much defiance –  she always looked for peaceful solutions –  and after two patient years she was given two days there, with the people she could relate to. I imagine she was hardly missed at Charlotte Street, but two days she was allowed, and that's what she had. Later Alicia was given almost complete freedom to visit, when it appeared no harm was being done, but her mother-in-law Georgina would not visit Bristol again until Phillipa was gone, and even then with reluctance – her son would never be welcoming.

: : :

Phillipa Anna Elena Rossetti's seventy-six years came to an end on a bright afternoon in June 1914, a month before war broke out. She died walking with her grandson along the Mardyke, falling to her knees clutching her chest and dying more or less in his arms – more or less because the event was dramatised in the *True Account* to such an extent that it's hard to believe any of it. But we know he was with her when she died. It was also near the spot where Thomas Grant, the hapless disgraced sailor, was found that morning in 1860, floating face-down in the dirty water with a bullet in his head. Fate, or just coincidence. Her grandson took her by rail to the crematorium at Woking, as she'd precisely ordered, then brought her all the way back to be scattered to the winds over Brandon Hill – an unexpected touch from someone usually empty of such sentiments... but I do know that the troubled Marquess of Queensbury was also cremated at Woking, and that he was much admired by her (he was known for his brutality and atheism –  but, seemingly ignored by her, also known for his deathbed conversion to Catholicism. We can all take the parts of other people's lives that appeal to us I guess, and overlook those that don't).

My father describes her death for us, then forgets his tenses and slips briefly into comedy: *"My Grandmother was laid out in Great Dignity in Our Front Room. With her usual Thoroughness, she described to me Her Wishes regarding Her Funeral, and I was much Honoured to carry Them out exactly as She asked. For all My future years, as I passed over Brandon Hill, I was reminded of that Illustrious Lady."*

That illustrious and thorough lady apparently left no instructions as to who should attend her funeral, so it was my father who decided not to object to anyone, it seems; his parents Georgina and Arthur made the journey, to mix with the quality people of Bristol, the wealthy shipowners and traders who'd known her and her ways. A bittersweet occasion perhaps, with the bitter part (I suspect) reserved for my father alone, to contrast with his mother's own lack of bitterness but abundance of sad memories of her wretched mother, the brazen, almost-friendless Phillipa Rossetti. You see that I have no affection for her, even in death.

Phillipa's final sin was not to take all her sins with her; instead she left them to her grandson, who thus inherited Rossetti Shipping & Trading, the company he'd effectively been running since a few years after his marriage. As war broke out in Europe, he renamed the company *The Bennett Line,* preferring no doubt to see his own name in lights rather than his grandmother's. He also sold *William & Rose* and *Roderick,* both old ships by then, and bought the almost-new *North Star,* the ship that would enthral me, and finally carry him to his death.

As years go, 1914 was the most eventful by far: a World War and The Bennett Line began, two ships were sold, and North Star was bought... Phillipa Rossetti died, and also my poor never-met brother Peter –  his death a tragedy made worse by my father, who could not, or would not, cope with it. Young Peter was six years old, and died two days after falling down Phillipa's once-private staircase at Charlotte Street. He never came out of his coma.

Phillipa was two months dead, and my father was in his study upstairs, as ever preoccupied with his business. Alicia was outside the house, showing Georgina the garden, and the boy was thought to be loosely in the care of his father –  the father who doted on him. The boy's clumping about suddenly ended with a clattering, followed by silence. His son had fallen from the top of the stairs to the bottom, and it was on his watch, as much as Alicia's. If there was to be any blame, it was equally his. Peter would surely have been tough enough for his father –  even in death he would eclipse me – but he was taken away from him, and it was everybody's fault except his own. His bellowing brought the women in, and my mother, pregnant with me, was all but thrashed by him in his fury. They had to fight to get the child away, in the face of his anger... he seemed more concerned, they said, with placing blame than with getting help for him. My grandmother Georgina described an extraordinary scene, with my so-called capable father beside himself and unable to help, shouting alongside his wife and his mother as they carried the boy away. Bad memories – of the event for them, and of the telling for me.

My father's wrath would never subside over his son's death, and the two women would have to suffer occasional bouts of being reminded of that day, and of how they could have avoided it if only they'd been doing their duty. A big man shouting at you is hard to reason with.

Three months after that day, still in 1914, I was born – a spindly travesty of a son and not a match for the lost one, but he named me Peter anyway. It seems that had his first son survived I would have been *Matthew*, after John Cabot's famous Bristol ship which crossed the North Atlantic in 1497, an endeavour much-loved by my father. But his pride for his own name pushed Matthew into second place for me – I was dropped into my dead brother's shoes and unknowingly took over the responsibility of bringing honour to the name Peter Bennett. If I had been a girl, who knows?

: : :

My uncle Richard went to sea properly, and to war, in the summer of 1915. I have no memory of him, just a photograph, looking proud in his gold-braided Lieutenant's uniform. Georgina and Arthur saw him off from Chepstow Station as he left for Portsmouth and the battle cruiser HMS *Black Prince;* James Armstrong, his old friend from Clifton, joined him en route, at Bristol. Richard sent a letter every month, the last one in mid-May 1916 when B*lack Prince* was part of the British Grand Fleet, and on the last day of that month they went with her across the North Sea towards Denmark into what became the Battle of Jutland. They never returned. They were among the six thousand British seamen who died there, *Black Prince* going down with its entire crew of eight hundred and fifty-seven, just around midnight on the first day of the battle. No bodies were recovered. They were gone, with nothing to give back to their families, lives simply ended without trace. Richard and James were both thirty-two, and older than most of the crew.

The Inn at Brockweir was a sad place to be in the weeks following Jutland. Georgina and Arthur had lost all three of their children, and the one still living sent a short letter of condolence; a brother was gone who was also a good friend, and his words were the best he could manage in his sadness. Georgina would always treasure the letter, especially the last line: *My thoughts are at Brockweir, with my family.* Alicia had brought his letter with her and she spent a month at the Inn, until the heavy veil of grief lifted a little and life picked itself up again. I was left at Charlotte Street in the close care of a nurse who, along with my father, would observe me carefully. My uncle Richard and his friend James were gone, and I knew nothing of it.

As I grew beyond babyhood, The Bennett Line continued to flourish. *North Star* and *Angel* would be joined by a larger ship (but still short enough to get around the bends in the Avon) named *Christian G,* soon renamed *Bennett Voyager.* She arrived in 1923, the year before this story begins, and was for one cargo only – tobacco – and while many others brought it to Avonmouth and barged it down the river to the harbour, Bennett Voyager took it directly to the wharves where it was taken straight to the huge bonded warehouses. Three of those buildings are still there today, but the tobacco has long gone.

My father stayed with *North Star,* and took just about any cargo that would fit: sherry from Spain, wine from Australia, as well as tobacco, cotton, sugar, molasses, fresh fruits, cocoa, – all from the West Indies and the eastern seaboard of North America, and sometimes timber, of all shapes and species, from the tropics, and from Canada and the Baltic. He enjoyed the variety of his cargoes, and going out from Bristol would take new Austin cars and Ferguson tractors to Ireland and the United States, and sometimes New Zealand, as well as steam coal from Cardiff or Barry when the price was right. The old Port was running down slowly, and would be truly viable only for ten years or so after the war. Avonmouth was pitiless, taking most of the trade from the mid thirties onwards, but whether or not my father was concerned, I don't know. Maybe he had plans to consolidate, or even go into the coastal trade like most other companies would.

He was certainly thinking of changes, however. In 1934, and shortly before his mother Georgina died, he'd told her he would be looking for someone to replace the hopeless people he had to leave the Business to, namely my mother and myself. We were not much offended; neither of us had any ambitions for *The Bennett Line,* but we hoped for a happy ending if and when it came. As for me, I would never have agreed to run that Company, even if I'd had the wit to do so; he would leave it to me at his peril, or, as it turned out, by default thirteen years after his death.

In my memory of him, which runs from the middle of the first war up to my leaving home in 1932, he was always at sea with *North Star,* and very rarely home. Not a reliable memory, but his time at home with us was short. He was not one for sitting in the office, as he once was, so left that to others while he travelled; his presence was always felt at the Mardyke offices however, and woe be to anyone letting his attention wander beyond those walls, or not following the Company line. He was in radio contact every day, and always had the fearsome demeanour I remember so well – his ships and his Business were run tightly and he was in charge, from wherever in the world he was. The Company line, and the way he ran his life, had not changed since his grandmother's death: have your way, no matter who gets in your way. A successful businessman – though little liked – but a very unsuccessful family man, and liked even less for that.

I remember a particular time, in the late thirties, after an almost-heated exchange and being far too grown-up to be hit by him, when I'd felt the need to defend my mother. I said, rather deeply, "You can't make love to a slave."

He was baffled. "What?"

I said it again.

He said, "What's the matter with you? It's none of your business. She's my wife, not a slave."

"You treat her like a slave. You know nothing about love."

He glared at me, turned and left. And then, because I expected a battle but he just walked away, I felt foolish and regretted what I'd said. I felt I'd hurt him when all I'd wanted in my heart was to make him think. I was naïve, as ever. Maybe my point was made, but I couldn't ever relate to my father, nor really win any fight with him.

Georgina and Arthur kept their distance from the affairs at Bristol, quietly running *The Wondrous Gift*, out of touch with their estranged son. They had no feedback, and it felt as though the family were split into two quite separate factions, twenty-five miles apart and never talking to each other, each unaware of the other's circumstances. It was hard for Georgina in the early years after Richard's death, not to hear from Peter – but the years passed and the silence became normal. She never wrote to him, instead clinging to the soft letter he'd written in 1916, keeping that memory alive. Anything from him now would no doubt be harsher, so she kept her son as she wanted him, and shied away from inviting change.

For Arthur, it was odd to know that his own name was attached to a shipping line, of all things, and very unreal when he thought back to his humbler beginnings at

Monmouth. His father had died just after the war, and his mother two years later. I remember the last time I saw his mother Lilian, at Christmas 1920 when I was six, and my bewilderment at her own bewilderment; she had become very vague – senile I guess – and I sat with my mother, opposite her above the shop as she looked around the room, smiling. Her bright beady eyes mostly stared into space, but with the smile, a wide vacant unreal smile which sometimes briefly left for a look of surprise, her eyebrows shooting upwards, her eyes goggling as if taking fright, before settling back to the smile. She had been a kind and caring woman all her life, yet suddenly she was so different, unreachable and cruelly comical, and it mystified me, and made me sad.

Their little shop in Church Street, where Arthur had grown up, stayed empty, locked and dark and dusty, for seven years before he could bear to part with it. There were no siblings to help him with the decision, and his wife allowed him his peace while privately lamenting the waste and the reluctance to move on – she was not the best example for him in that... moving on is largely a private matter, as she would have known. The empty building became a hardware shop, and Arthur insisted on using most of the money he got from the sale on improvements to the Inn – he redecorated some of the rooms, and put in a proper car park in front – the days of the horse were ending, and the nineteen-twenties saw a huge rise in motor vehicles; as well as regular traffic, tourism was on the rise, and weekends especially were very busy in the Wye Valley. Parking was needed, and he was proud to provide it from his own money.

They were both in their sixties then, and feeling tired with the continuous work of running the Inn – incidentally now referred to as *The Hotel,* which sounded better to them, and more upmarket. They made the decision to hand over the work, and advertised in the *Monmouthshire Beacon* for "A Competent Manager, to reside at The Hotel, and to take charge of the daily management of all necessary matters, and of the Staff." Two weeks later, Alfred Evans, formerly manager at the Kings Head Hotel in Monmouth, arrived and immediately took the weight from their shoulders. They were relieved and released, free to spend their days as they wished, all the while fretfully casting their eyes over Alfred's methods.

In 1932, the year I first came back from college, I called in at Brockweir to see my grandparents and Georgina talked at length to me about her son, my father Peter. She had bad memories of her mother Phillipa and of the effect she'd had on Peter, and was trying to settle everything in her mind. All the old memories she'd pushed away had come back in her old age. It was a mess. Things done many years ago could not be unravelled, and she struggled even to express how she felt. Her life at Charlotte Street, her escape, the ensnaring of her son and then his turning against her, the loss of their first, and last child... none of it could be put right. I was helpless, and the two of us talked in private for several hours (Arthur was elsewhere), she simply telling me everything about those long-ago times. I naively thought she wanted my advice (I would have had none to give) but all she wanted was a listener, I think. Arthur returned and I was glad to sit with them both again; when I left them later that day in my borrowed car for Bristol and my mother, they waved after me, looking frail and tired, arms linked, at the roadside. My grandmother Georgina was seventy-two, a year younger than Arthur, and I would see her just once more, the following year; she would leave us for ever a year after that, in 1934.

: : :

The second War came, and in early 1942 my father was into the routine of the Atlantic convoys. The Bennett Line ticked over in Bristol with coastal work: imports brought south from Liverpool, exports from Bristol to Ireland and the Thames, but the dangerous North Atlantic was avoided along with the North Sea routes to the Baltic – all out of bounds for *Bennett Voyager*. *Angel* had been sold by then.

Captain Bennett chose to take *North Star* into the Battle of the Atlantic, into the most perilous situation of a convoy spread across the sea-lanes, albeit under the protection of the Royal Navy. He was unlucky, and the fourteenth of May brought the news that my mother had truly dreaded, and she took it with her usual stoicism. She grieved, but also struggled with the unfamiliar rising joy of being liberated at last, freed from this man who'd never properly valued her since their wedding, and these mixed feelings would torment her in the months after. She lived with the sadness, and the hesitant, almost-guilty release of something kept inside for so long. At fifty-eight, she had some good years left, and although the ghost of my father stayed with her I believe she did often allow herself to be joyous – genuinely so. As time passed she softened her memories of her husband, thinking better of him, and this helped her keep the bitterness at bay. Only in her last years did she again struggle with life, as the old memories came back with their sadnesses, in the same way Georgina's had.

## 17

## MY QUIET REVENGE

My wife Clara had moved into Charlotte Street with my mother in 1942 after my father's death, and following the war we all lived there, bringing up our two children while both producing the art that was our living. Patrick was born in 1946, Elena three years later, and my mother Alicia was happy for us all to share the house with her. She sometimes enjoyed herself with cooking, an unknown talent she'd discovered during the war when her cook left. She shared the house with Clara and the housekeeper until I returned in 1945, and still enjoyed providing for us all now and then, even after a new cook was taken on. I can imagine her husband's horror at the thought of his wife actually preparing food for the cook, the housekeeper, and everyone else. Although her two employees would always eat separately from the family, they were occasionally, rarely, cooked for by their employer, an undreamt-of situation we all wondered at... but why not? Her husband's death was allowing her to live.

Arthur Bennett had also died in April 1942, just a month before his son, after living his last eight years in Monmouth near his old home in Church Street. Captain Bennett was at sea, and missed the funeral; I wonder how sad he was to lose his father, after denouncing him for most of his life. His mother Georgina (my lovely grandmother) had died in 1934 and he'd come with my mother to her small funeral at Tintern, but was as remote as ever with his family, the perfect example of an important businessman not having quite enough time for people he thought inferior, not even his grieving father. He'd filled us all with degrees of sadness or anger, depending on how well we'd known him.

Arthur had moved into town soon after the funeral, leaving the Hotel in the hands of Alfred Evans and his staff. He owned everything at Brockweir, and in his will gave it all to me, no doubt sad not to be happy for his son to have it, nor his daughter-in-law Alicia. I was to be the one, and Alicia, my mother, thought it fitting. I knew I would one day inherit everything else, *The Bennett Line* included, and I knew even then what I would do with it. The Floating Harbour, the old *Float*, held no interest for me beyond the memories of my childhood there, and I gave no positive thought to my father's – my family's – business. It was all out of mind, and nothing changed after his death, my mother simply delegating everything and not involving me at all. My fear of the water and small boats has not left me, and I'm content never to have been physically involved in ships and the sea: memories of my *North Star,* and many sea-dreams, have been enough.

My father never made a will. After all his experience and dealings with business, he never got round to it, and his precious company went to his wife; but who else would there have been? Just me, his pathetic son. It would be traumatic for him, to see his hard work going to someone as passive as his wife. The replacement someone he'd told his mother about in 1934 had materialised six years later as a Bristolian, Benjamin Poole, and if my father had finalised matters before leaving on that convoy in 1942, things would I'm sure be different now. As it was, Benjamin Poole was involved, but not a part of the business, and after my father's memorial service (at Sandhurst Church, where he was married) he spoke frankly with my mother, telling her of her husband's plans to cut her out – which didn't surprise her at all. She'd quietly drifted through the years, aware of his dismissal of any uses she had, and suspected a change of course when her favourite *Angel* was sold, and not replaced. The money would be needed, she was told, that's all. That was 1939, and *Angel*'s by then diminishing profits were halted by her sale; Alicia was told nothing, but the changes around her in the Port, and the coming war, suggested a scaling-down, perhaps. In the following years Captain Bennett would be busy with the war effort, so his not-to-be associate Benjamin Poole came and went, without bothering anyone.

*The Bennett Line,* and its sole survivor *Bennett Voyager,* were managed from then on by my father's favourite, George Watson. He'd been manager for ten years or more, keeping things sweet at the Mardyke office while his boss was far away, and after some anxiety he agreed to carry on without that boss, and without *North Star,* in the competent way he'd carried on before, working now for my mother. We wondered how devoted he actually was to my father, and how much respect he had for him, especially in view of the many aggressive radio calls he'd had to deal with over the years. The running of the Business was left entirely to him, his salary improved, and life went on there without a hiccup. Captain Peter Bennett was missed, but not that much; my mother certainly grieved but beyond hers there weren't many tears shed in Bristol, apart from mine – and mine were not for the flesh and blood father I knew.

After the war George Watson suggested that another ship be found, a smaller vessel for fetching and carrying around the coasts of Britain – my mother agreed (in a rare moment of delight in actually being asked) and allowed him to find one. *Prince Alfred* arrived in autumn 1946, a week before our son Patrick was born (we were both thirty-two then, and after my safe return from war we'd decided to have children. The fear of a fatherless child had been stronger than the need we'd felt for a family, so we waited, with no idea at the time of how long that wait would be).

When news of the new ship reached Brockweir, *Prince Alfred* became Alfred Evans's unofficial name amongst his staff, which he never seemed to mind. The Hotel staff were always interested in what happened at Bristol, of the family's ups and downs, and far from being shy would ask me for updates whenever I visited them. I suppose I was softer than most bosses, but the unwanted muse of my father was always over me, telling me not to be stupid, so I was happy to frustrate him.

: : :

My mother Alicia was seventy when she died, in 1955. I felt so sorry for her, so sad to see her go, after a life of subjection which changed little after her husband died. Even the times when she could have defended me against him but didn't, I forgive, because of the outright fear she had of him. It's true she had her times of respite, of happiness, with her family around her – but they were short, and few. With more years, she could have won more freedom from him, perhaps. I shall remember her when she was happy, with her grandchildren on Brandon Hill on summer days, and in the snow, walking across the windy hill high above the harbour. And always her cooking – she was happy then.

She died of pneumonia, a wasteful death that could surely have been prevented – and I became wealthy, from an overnight inheritance before its time, brought on by the Bristol rain that soaked her and led to a cold, to a fever, and to her death, the same progression that had killed Phillip Rossetti so long before.

I was wealthy, for sure.

In the weeks after, *The Bennett Line* was legally given to me, the one person who could never make anything of it, according to my father. So I prepared to make nothing of it, proving him right. My mother had said to me the year before, "You may do what you like with this business, when I'm gone", and the wait for her to go was painfully short. She'd had no function, no say, in the business. She was the Captain's wife and my mother, that's all.

After her death I basked in an interlude both bitter and sweet, but *The Bennett Line* had run its course and I accepted her offer and did what I liked. I fear many good (and dead) people turned to me with hate in their eyes for that – they would have despised me for it, I'm sure. All except one or two, perhaps: Phillip Rossetti would understand, and also John Parrish. After all the defilement of their labours by those who followed them, I believe they would both forgive me for this, for my attempt to keep their efforts alive but ending the progress that came after. Their particular time is kept clear, and unsullied.

My mother died, and I had my sale, which I took no time at all in bringing about: a sale of stock, of machines, of methods – I shifted a weight of ships and people from my mind. The Company Manager, George Watson, far from being of my father's sort, turned out to be a good man. He was sixty when the Company was wound up, and although sad to see it all go, realised that Bristol was changing faster than he could have adapted to it. He was well rewarded, along with the staff at the Mardyke and the crews of *Prince Alfred* and *Bennett Voyager*, most of whom,

I think, found other work. It couldn't be helped; it was gone, over with, and I was glad.

My mother was buried at her family's church at Sandhurst, a return to the place and the people she'd loved before her husband's time. Her parents had gone by then and her brother, whom I'd met just twice before, spoke quietly of her life of service to a man who failed to see her qualities. The funeral was easy, a beautiful summer's afternoon for her to leave us all. I think everyone was grateful she'd had some years without him, even while realising he'd never really left her; thirty-six years with someone is a long time, but the thirteen without him were not enough, even when filled with the distractions of her son, his wife, and grandchildren.

So the day went well, but we came home feeling the loss of a friend, and the house was emptier because of her. She'd loved our children, and fussed endlessly over them. Patrick was nine when she died, and already leaning towards his eventual career of accountancy (a more alien occupation for myself I couldn't imagine, but he loved numbers as much as his parents loved colours, so how could we object?). Elena was more reflective, a sad six-year-old then, and who still treasures the pictures she'd made for her grandmother just before her short illness.

They both went through school almost uneventfully, and after five years that felt like a lifetime, we decided to leave Bristol and settle near the Hotel in the Wye Valley – Elena was eleven, and would start her secondary school time at Monmouth, and Patrick at fourteen wasn't daunted by a change to Monmouth Boy's School. He was always bolder than I ever was... just a few stray genes from my father, no doubt. Eighteen Charlotte Street went to a new owner, and was perhaps the hardest to part with, but I wanted nothing solid left of me in Bristol.

We moved in August 1960 to a spacious bungalow surrounded by fields, at the bottom of the straggling village of Whitebrook on the old road to Monmouth and a long stone's throw, across gently sloping meadows, from the River Wye. It was a complete novelty for us all after the stone and traffic of Bristol. *Lower Barn* was not a barn at all, and never had been; it was only twenty years old but on the site of a very old farm, all traces long gone, apart from the inappropriate name. We decided to change that name, as none of us could imagine anything further removed from a barn, so we thought about alternatives: we went through all the usual favourites, from *Greenfields* to *Riverside*, from *New House* to Elena's fanciful *Bright Haven*. We gave them all up though, after a neighbour told us of the old Welsh name for the long-disappeared farm – *Celyn*, which means *holly*; and sure enough, we found at least three holly trees in our boundary hedges, so the name *Celyn* returned to Lower Whitebrook.

18

## FINAL THOUGHTS

*The Wondrous Gift* has been a successful venture. From Phillip Rossetti's day, through the immense changes of the Industrial Revolution, from King George, via William, Victoria, a couple of Edwards and more Georges, to Queen Elizabeth. Big changes, but through them all the Hotel has quietly prospered and changed little; Phillip would recognise everything even now, the rooms, even most of the décor, and certainly the view from his window across the river. My daughter Elena is the owner, and will pass it on to her daughter Alice, in time.

In 1967, when Elena was eighteen, she'd decided against university. Her brother Patrick had moved to Cheltenham, working for an accountancy firm, and appeared to be set on his particular path. Elena had other ideas: she would forego her degree (just as her daughter would, in the years ahead) and give her life to *The Wondrous Gift*, our beloved Hotel, our Inn, and began by leaving us and moving in there to learn the business, persuading us to employ her.

She would work with Alfred Evans, then beyond retirement age, and the timing was good; we were all impressed with her, and three years later, at twenty-one, she was given the deeds and became the owner, as Alfred left. To keep the fairness, Patrick was given the value of the Hotel, and was more than happy.

In 1969 Elena had met and married David Lindberg, a teacher of English from Cleddon, a village in the forest above Brockweir, whom she'd met at her school reunion a year before; he was five years older than her, and a calming influence on her sometimes untamed ambitions for *The Wondrous Gift*. She wanted to change the image of the place, which was alarming to Clara and me, but her ideas of change settled down to room décor and menus; the rooms became brighter, the food more interesting, and the rest stayed as it was. We breathed again, after questioning our judgement; it would have been too late though, and we would have lived with whatever came, just about. David was very supportive to her, while keeping his work at Monmouth School.

After owning the Hotel for six months, a short half-year in which she'd piled up the responsibilities and routines to a precarious level, Elena became pregnant. Suddenly life became difficult for her. It was unplanned and threatened to throw her off course, but after a week or so of berating herself she decided to carry on, to continue her pregnancy even though she could have ended it. Her husband was relieved, both for the child and for her keeping to her ambitions, but it was hard, and she did well to stay on top of everything. An unexpected child usually derails things – plans are changed, targets are reset, life is rearranged – and Elena's life at the Hotel was briefly derailed. We were delighted with the coming child, yet dared not say so at the beginning – but as the months passed Elena became as happy as we were, when she could see the road ahead smoothing out for her. We were all involved in that, David especially making sure the staff would help her when necessary, even when she didn't want help... a delicate trick, and not always appreciated. Elena, and everyone else, looked forward to the autumn and the accidental child – she was to be my only grandchild, Alice Rossetti Lindberg.

: : :

My life changed in probably the biggest way ever, when I lost Clara, suddenly and inexplicably, in 1988. *The beat of my heart for thirty years,* as someone once said, but with her it was closer to fifty; she was seventy-four, and it was too soon. She went before me and therefore without me, and nine years have not faded her in my memory – quite the opposite: often in my studio I have one-sided conversations with her, easy and indulgent episodes amongst the familiar clutter of art that was our lives, her bright landscapes balancing my endless procession of faces. In my time I've painted portraits of my mother and grandmother from life, and my father from memory, but Clara, best of all, and many times – an evolving series of images which still show her exactly as the painter saw her. She left me with those portraits and of all her likenesses the best for me is the last one, the one that showed her full of all her life. At nineteen, when I first knew her, there was beauty and innocence, but at seventy-four there was beauty and enlightenment; I knew her, and I understood her. I'll move on, but it's a strange place to be, this growing old, where the people you've known all your life are leaving it, one by one.

And growing old is not something that troubles the young, but they have their own, different, problems. My granddaughter Alice, at the moment, is one of those whose lives are not smooth. She's helped me greatly with this history and I wish she could feel better about life. I know she will one day forgive me for mentioning this, but she's a different Alice to the one we used to have, and I look forward to having her back.

I should have mentioned the arrival of someone very special who came to the Hotel in 1971, after Elena had searched far and wide for a good example of an African

Grey Parrot, the very image of The Wondrous Gift on the signboard. Aku returned to us as if from the dead, from Phillip Rossetti's days. Elena was insistent on finding him and putting back *the missing piece of the Hotel,* as she put it, and she called him Aku in honour of his celebrated ancestor. He was kept in Elena's bedroom at the front of the Hotel, as the original Aku had been, but nowadays he's moved down to the bottom of the stairs to allow Alice and Jon the front rooms, with Phillip's old bedroom and study.

Alice, Aku's mistress, has succeeded in getting him to come to the broom, but only indoors. She lacks the courage so far, it seems, to allow him outside; I think it's just a matter of time.

So that's how things are now, and I'm happy that the Hotel is going well. It seems our girls have become proper hotel owners, the last thing I expected of them. I shall keep watching, from a distance, while hoping that nothing upsets their balance.

Now I'm almost done with this story, and I'll finish it by going back, a final goodbye to the life I had in Bristol. The city is an old friend, a detached place with a life's memories, and sometimes a soft light falls on one or other of those memories and reminds me of something good, which is a blessing. The bad ones have faded, and gradually huddled towards the back of my mind since I cut my ties there those forty years ago, and even though this story has called most of them out again, I manage, and Bristol remains close to me.

I drive up the hill and look along Charlotte Street, without turning into it; I stop the traffic for a moment, and look along the street – our house is there, sitting in the afternoon sun, looking out over the harbour, but I drive on. The City is roads and views to me now, and I usually drive around rather than walk on the ground I grew up on. The Hotwell Road is a sad favourite, along the old Mardyke, past the place where a young boy went out in a small boat many years ago and broke with his father. My old dreaming-place under Brunel's bridge has long gone, lost somewhere beneath the tarmac of the Portway road.

There are very few people left alive here – apart from a few special friends – who remember me, or the Company I briefly owned, or the ships that came and went. And I know no one who remembers my father. He is gone, lost, a faded memory even for me – but what I did was because of him; he was alive in my mother for thirteen years after his death, and he made me wait for her life of quiet heroism to be over before I had my indulgence, the vengeful act of which I am most definitely guilty: I got rid of the hallowed Family Business that began in Genoa, two hundred years before. But more to the point, it was the end of *The Bennett Line*. That was my revenge on him – and his grandmother – and I've lived happily ever after.

*Well, my anger shows.*

After all I've said about trying to find love for him, this is how it ends, in revenge. Could I have tried harder? If affection was what he needed, why couldn't I find some for him? I can't resolve this. Oscar Wilde said, 'Each man kills the thing he loves', and I wonder whether that's what my father did, with me, and that led to me doing it to him. I'll spend the rest of my life on that one, because it's not true to say I've lived entirely happily since his death – it seems to me the important people in our lives never quite leave us, and I'm sure my father will be with me for the remainder of mine. So I try to finish here with him, but leave that revenge in place.

I shall pack up the heavy ledgers, the invoices, the scribbled notes: I've used them all in this story, and they will be kept here, at *Celyn*, for whoever comes after me with a curiosity that needs satisfying. Pietro's journal, Phillip's sparse diary and John Parrish's letters, I also keep here, but on my bookshelves along with the few treasured photographs. I've finished with the *True Account,* taken what I've needed and put it aside, and as it sits on my bookshelf it will have a note inside the cover –

*Beware, for there are lies among the truths.*

Whoever reads it must, as I did, sort out the good from the bad. My endeavours have been personal, and my interpretations somewhat biased. My father was responsible for that, because of the harm he did to my mother and to me, and to many others, and his words will be ripples on water, spreading the false and the true to be received as false or true by the finder, who already I envy for his or her detachment and lack of experience. Make of it what you will. It's a great story. Accept it all if you wish, and adjust what is already believed, but the past really is solid – history cannot be changed, just the rendition of it, so Phillip Rossetti's home will keep its truths and its quiet connections with Bristol. This personal history of mine will endure or be lost, and either is fine with me. It was the writing of it that mattered.

I'm living now for my ever-unmarried son Patrick, my daughter Elena and her David, and of course Alice and Jon, hoping they experience the love I shared with Clara, and not the pretence of love my father gave to my mother. My story is over, and I shall wait out my life here.

*Celyn, Saturday, February 22nd 1997*

THANK YOU to my wife Evi for her unfailing support,
and for providing the word 'UPRIVER',
which gave me the initial idea for my novel
*The Gentle River*
– and for this book, in its turn

Thanks also to Edward and Marian Drzymalski
for introducing me to Aku, and his ways

: : :

*Read my novel*
*THE GENTLE RIVER*
*which is framed around the*
*history presented here*

*Also*
*SEVEN SHORT STORIES*

*Details at  www.gordonwilliams.uk*

*REFERENCES*

The Merchant Seamen of Bristol 1747-1789
*Jonathan Press, 1976, Ed. Peter Harris*
*The Historical Association, Bristol Branch*

Bristol Shipbuilding in the Nineteenth Century
*Grahame Farr, 1971, Ed. Peter Harris*
*The Historical Association, Bristol Branch*

Life in Victorian Bristol
*Helen Reid, Redcliffe Press, 2005*

Bristol Times Revisited
*David Harrison, The History Press, 2014*

Images of Maritime Bristol
*Paul Elkin, Breedon Books, 1995*

A City Built Upon the Water,
Maritime Bristol 1750-1900
*Ed. Steve Poole, Redcliffe Press, 2013*

Brunel, the Man Who Built the World
*Steven Brindle, Weidenfeld & Nicolson, 2005*

Charles Heath's Proud Days for Monmouth
*Nelson Museum & Local History Centre, Monmouth,*
*Facsimile Reprint, 2002*

Bristol's Floating Harbour: The First 200 Years
*Peter Malpass & Andy King, Redcliffe Press, 2009*